GARRISON'S
GORILLAS

GARRISON'S GORILLAS
and the Fear Formula

Authorized Edition
based on the popular
television series

by JACK PEARL

Illustrated by HARVEY KIDDER

WHITMAN PUBLISHING DIVISION
WESTERN PUBLISHING COMPANY, INC., RACINE, WISCONSIN

CONTENTS

1   Formula 1-X   11

2   A Taste of Terror   20

3   Assignment Kropotkin   31

4   Ambush   45

5   Journey With Tigers   61

6   End of the Line   75

7   A Laboratory Prison   92

8   Casey Gets a Job   111

9   The Strange Set of Twins   121

10   Break-Out!   133

11   The Real Emile   149

12   Attack in Darkness   162

13   Don't Drink Anything!   172

14   At Balzer's Cottage   182

15   The Mighty Men   195

1.

FORMULA 1-X

THE NAZI OFFICERS kept glancing impatiently at their watches. One of the two plainclothes Gestapo agents present in the laboratory growled at Professor Jules Kropotkin.

"How much longer?"

"I told you it will take fifteen minutes for the injection to take effect," Kropotkin replied coldly. The internationally famous Czechoslovakian scientist did not try to conceal his hatred for his Nazi captors.

Kropotkin's native land had been transformed into one gigantic concentration camp by Hitler's occupation troops. His personal prison was a Nazi experimental lab set up in a big country house which had once belonged to a high Czech diplomat, in the woods on the outskirts of Prague.

Jules Kropotkin was a big, brawny man with sparse blond hair. He looked like a football player rather than a biological scientist. His blue eyes were fixed on a big striped alley cat curled up in one corner of a metal cage sitting on a table in the middle of the room. The cat was licking its paws contentedly.

"All right," Kropotkin said finally. "It is time." He removed a white mouse from a cage at the side of the lab and carried it over to the table. Opening a trapdoor on top of the cat's cage, he dropped the mouse inside.

The Germans crowded close around the table, watching expectantly. They were not disappointed. The white mouse crouched where the professor had dropped it, its pink eyes beady with terror. But it was not the stricken mouse that held the men's attention. It was the cat.

Yowling with fear, it pressed itself flat against the side of the cage as far away from the rodent as it could get. Its back was arched, the fur on its spine bristling. Its tail was a fat balloon.

"Incredible!" whispered one of the Gestapo men. "It seems to be mad with fear."

"It is," Kropotkin said. "Watch this now."

The mouse, bewildered by the behavior of its most feared enemy, twitched its tail and scurried into a corner of the cage opposite the cat. At the sudden motion, the cat let out a plaintive wail and collapsed in a trembling mass on the floor of the cage.

The professor opened the trapdoor and removed the mouse from the cage. "I don't want the poor cat to die from heart failure," he explained.

All of the Germans were talking at once in excited voices.

"This is a momentous occasion, gentlemen," General Schwartz of the General Staff in Berlin exclaimed. "Wait until the *Führer* hears of it. Think of it! A drug that can turn a whole nation into a population of sniveling cowards."

"Please, General, let me speak." Colonel Dorne, the medical officer in charge of the laboratory, held up his hands for silence. "It will not be that easy."

General Schwartz frowned, his thick Prussian neck swelling red inside his tight collar. "What are you talking about, Colonel? I read the official report on this serum." He tapped a fat finger on a folder on the table. Big black letters read: FEAR 1-x—TOP SECRET.

"It states that just one quart of the formula can contaminate the water supply of a city of one million people. A few ounces can convert a division of brave soldiers into blubbering ninnies. Already, successful tests have been conducted in two small French villages."

14

"Yes, what are we waiting for?" his aide, Colonel Braun, demanded. "Our agents in England can get to work as soon as we supply them with Fear One-X. They can begin with the water supplies around the big army encampments."

"But that's just it, gentlemen," Colonel Dorne said miserably. "We cannot supply them with the serum at this time."

"And why not?" Schwartz asked.

"Because this is our entire supply of Fear One-X," Jules Kropotkin cut in. He was leaning back against his laboratory workbench, holding up a beaker of thick, milky liquid. A sly smile played over his face. "Less than six ounces, *Herr* General."

General Schwartz looked at Colonel Dorne in confusion. "I don't understand."

Colonel Dorne sighed and wiped a hand across his gleaming bald head. "The fact is, sir, that Jules Kropotkin here is only one half of the research team that developed the serum. He and his brother Emile were working on it as a joint project even as our glorious leader's troops were at the gates of Prague."

"At the order of our government, Emile and I destroyed all of our secret files," Kropotkin said, clearly enjoying the story and the frustration he saw on the Germans' faces. "The formula for the serum is extremely complicated. There are two processes, really. I memorized the first part of the formula. Emile memorized the second part—the most important part, the catalytic refining formula. The day the Germans entered Prague we shook hands and went our different ways. I haven't seen my brother since."

General Schwartz scowled at Dorne. "How do we know he's telling the truth?"

"Oh, it's the truth, all right," the colonel assured him. "Jules and Emile Kropotkin have published papers in medical journals all over the world. They worked in utter seclusion, refused to grant interviews or have their photographs taken.

But it is a matter of record that they were working together on this project when war broke out in Europe. Jules Kropotkin was picked up in a matter of weeks by our agents. But German intelligence has been scouring the Continent for nineteen months without picking up Emile's trail. There is very little to go on, as I told you. Not even a photograph of the man."

General Schwartz pointed an irate finger at Kropotkin. "Wipe that smile off your face! What is so funny?"

"I was just thinking. Possibly Emile has fallen into the hands of the Russians, and they may have him locked up somewhere like this, trying to wring the formula out of him."

General Schwartz paled. "Is it possible?"

"No!" snapped a Gestapo man. "If Emile Kropotkin had been captured by the Russians, we would know it, just as the Allies know that we have his brother. We have confirmation, too, that an intensive search is under way in the resistance movement, aimed at finding Emile before we do."

"I see." The general stared at the beaker of precious serum in Kropotkin's hand. "He could still be lying," he said slowly. "Maybe Jules Kropotkin knows the entire formula himself."

"That possibility has been thoroughly explored and disproven," one of the Gestapo agents said grimly.

Kropotkin laughed bitterly. "Thoroughly explored." He put down the beaker and opened the front of his white lab jacket and his shirt, exposing his bare chest.

General Schwartz's face turned deep crimson as he gazed on the grillwork of partially healed scars that disfigured the professor's body.

"No, sir," Colonel Dorne said, "we will have to find Emile Kropotkin before we can manufacture enough Fear One-X serum for effective use against the Allies."

"He will be found!" General Schwartz

pounded his fist down on the table. His face was purple with rage as he turned to the two Gestapo agents. "Intelligence reports indicate that the English and the Americans intend to launch a massive invasion against the Continent before summer. That gives us less than three months to find Emile Kropotkin and produce sufficient Fear One-X to contaminate the Allies' water supplies. If he is not found, Hitler will have all of our heads!"

The Gestapo men, Colonel Dorne, and Colonel Braun snapped to attention and thrust their right arm high into the air.

"*Heil* Hitler!" they chorused.

Jules Kropotkin looked on with scornful amusement. To himself he said, *The pigs will never find my brother in a million years!*

2.

A TASTE
OF TERROR

THE EIGHTH AIR FORCE had had a field day over Berlin, with seven hundred bombers and fighter escorts taking part in one of the biggest daylight raids of the war. Casualties were high.

Maj. Mike Connors, flight leader of the 358th Fighter Squadron, had taken a hit in the tail assembly of his P-51 Mustang on the way out, making the ship very hard to control. Now he was limping back at quarter speed, far behind the main attack force, with only his wingman to cover him.

They almost made it.

Just forty miles from the French coastline two German Messerschmitt 109 fighters jumped them from out of the sun.

Connors' wingman, Capt. Paul Dale, put up a great battle, but he was restricted because he had to stay close to his disabled squadron commander.

Connors kept shouting at him over the radio: "Get the heck out of here, buddy! Save your own neck. It won't do the Eighth any good to lose both of us. I'm a dead pigeon anyway!"

Dale just ignored the order and took on both ME-109's single-handed. He nailed one with a deflection shot in the gas tank. A tracer shell exploded in the high octane fuel, and the German plane mushroomed into a ball of fire.

But the other Messerschmitt was right on his tail. Dale rolled and turned and dipped, with the German's tracers whistling all around the Mustang's canopy. Then a lucky burst from the Messerschmitt tore off his left wing. The P-51

21

flipped and nosedived like a wounded bird, and Dale barely managed to bail out and open his chute.

Now the German tore into Connors' helpless fighter. In seconds it, too, was spiraling down in a plume of black smoke.

Both Connors and Dale landed safely in a desolate wooded area. They had just buried their chutes, according to procedure, when three bearded men in French peasant dress came out of the forest, silent as ghosts. Dale went for his Colt automatic.

The man in the lead held up a hand and said in softly accented English, "We are friends. The maquis."

"The maquis?" Connors repeated. He pushed Dale's hand away from the gun at his waist. "The underground resistance movement," he said.

The Americans and the Frenchmen shook hands. "When it is dark we will take you to the coast, where a fishing boat will take you back to

England," the French leader, Pierre, informed them.

They sat down in a clearing and ate a meal of bread, cheese, and red wine. Afterward the fliers passed out American cigarettes, and they smoked and talked about the war.

One of the other Frenchmen nudged Pierre. "Tell the Americans about the bewitched village we came upon this morning."

Pierre's dark face scowled and there was fear in his eyes. "I don't even want to think of that accursed place."

"Bewitched village?" Connors grinned and winked at Dale. "Come on, Pierre," he urged. "Tell us about it. We like ghost stories."

The Frenchman stared at him somberly. "It is hard to tell. But we will take you there. It's only a few miles from here and on our way."

"Good." The major got to his feet eagerly. "It will be dark soon anyway."

It was dusk when they reached the edge of

the small rustic town. From the shadow of the trees Connors surveyed the main street, unusually deserted for so early in the evening.

"Any Germans here?" he asked.

"There were many Germans here until a few weeks ago," one of Pierre's men told him. "Before the village was cursed. Suddenly they all left."

Connors frowned. "Well, let's see this curse for ourselves."

With the major and Pierre in the lead, they walked down the main street. The place was eerily silent. No song. No laughter. No children's voices. Major Connors shivered, but it was not from the cold. The village had a strange feeling about it—as if it were indeed haunted!

As they passed by the houses he caught a furtive movement of curtain and blinds. Unseen eyes were peering out at them. Up ahead an old man and an old woman were huddled on their front porch. It was good to see some sign of life.

Pierre waved a friendly hand and called out

a greeting in French. The old couple began to whimper and shake. They scrambled up and into their house, as if the devil were on their heels, and bolted the door.

"What the heck is this, Mike?" Dale whispered. "This place gives me the creeps."

They were almost at the village square now. Ahead Connors saw a group of children sitting on the grass. They were crowded close together like timid sheep. Connors reached into his pocket and brought out a package of chewing gum. He opened it and fanned out the sticks. This was a language that children all over the world understood. Smiling as he approached them, he said in halting French, "Americans . . . friends . . . chewing gum. . . . We give you gum and chocolate, see?"

He saw them rise on their haunches like little animals poised to flee from danger. Their hungry eyes regarded the gum. It was plain they wanted it very badly. But there was something else in their faces, some emotion that Connors could not fathom. He stopped.

"Please don't run away," he said quietly. "We are friends. We won't harm you."

Just then a small bird swooped out of a tree and flew low over the square, chirping its evening song.

What happened after that, Major Connors would never forget. Screaming in hysteria, the children scattered in all directions. Connors had never before seen such terrible panic.

Pierre touched his arm. "You are satisfied, Major?" he asked quietly. "Is it not so that this village is bewitched?"

Connors and Dale exchanged looks, frightened by what each saw in the eyes of the other.

Forty-eight hours later Connors and Dale, none the worse for their close shave, were seated in the inner sanctum of Supreme Headquarters, Allied Expeditionary Forces, on the outskirts of

London, telling their story to a ring of serious, attentive faces. These men represented some of the highest ranking brass on General Dwight Eisenhower's staff. In addition, three English generals were present.

After two hours of intensive interrogation a colonel of the Intelligence Corps addressed the group somberly.

"The Kropotkin formula—there can be no doubt about it. The Nazis have used it on that village. And from what Connors and Dale have seen and described, the experiment was a total success—men, women, and children reduced to quaking cowards, almost demented with fear."

"What happens now?" an infantry general demanded. He squirmed uncomfortably. "For all we know, German agents may be poisoning the reservoirs that supply the water for our troops at this very moment."

The colonel grinned wryly. "No. Relax, General—for the time being. We've known about this project—Fear One-X is the German code name—for almost two years."

He briefed them on the case of the Kropotkins —how Jules had been captured with a small quantity of the deadly serum, how Emile had seemingly vanished from the face of the earth, how Nazi and Allied intelligence had been competing feverishly to locate the elusive Emile for nineteen months without success.

"What it amounts to is this," another general spoke up. "If the Germans find Emile before our side does, they will have the power to turn the Allied armies into mobs of helpless, frightened children!"

"That's about it," the colonel confirmed.

The highest ranking member of the military present, a four-star general, said crisply, "I am speaking for General Eisenhower when I tell you that it is time for our cloak-and-dagger boys to stop playing games. Emile Kropotkin must be found. *Quickly!* And by our side!"

"Sir," the intelligence colonel said defensively, "our best men have been knocking themselves out on this assignment for months. I don't know what else we can do."

"I do," the four-star general said sharply. "It's time to throw in the shock troops."

The colonel did not miss the emphasis on the word "shock." He winced. "You mean. . . ."

"Exactly! Garrison's Gorillas. If anyone can find Emile Kropotkin on the face of Europe, it's Craig Garrison and his bunch of cutthroats!"

3.

ASSIGNMENT KROPOTKIN

THE BEST DARNED guerrilla fighters in any man's army!" was how Craig Garrison described his men, although he had to admit there was more than a little "gorilla" in them, too.

First Lieutenant Garrison was a lithe, lean man with light brown hair and blue eyes that were as hard as flint. Garrison had packed more living into his relatively few years than most men do in a full lifetime. World War II was less than twenty-four hours old for the United States when he enlisted in the Army.

His first hitch was in the newly formed Rangers. He went in with the first wave in the Allied invasion of North Africa. He was one of the first ashore in Sicily, at Salerno. For two months he worked with the partisans behind the German lines in Italy. Then it was back to England where the Allies were massing for the big invasion of the Continent. There he was wounded twice in hit-and-run commando raids on the French coast to test Nazi defenses in Normandy.

During his short convalescence in an Army hospital, Garrison got the inspiration to form a fighting outfit of super-guerrilla soldiers, the like of which no army on earth had ever seen before.

His experience with the Italian partisans and the Rangers had taught Craig Garrison that the qualities that made a good guerrilla fighter might send a man to prison in civilian life. It took months of hard work to train a nice, civilized recruit—who may have been a respectable clerk, bank teller, or plumber before he joined the armed forces—to become a ruthless killer or to operate behind enemy lines blowing up bridges, cracking safes to get at secret documents, or picking a German officer's pockets. Sometimes it was impossible to teach a man things that he had always looked on as unlawful and bad.

Why not, Garrison wondered, enlist men who were professionals in these skills?

When he was released from the hospital, he outlined his idea to his commanding officer.

"The point is this, sir. They'll be doing the same things that got them into prison back in the States, only they'll be doing them against the Germans!"

His colonel liked the idea. So did the Pentagon. And "Garrison's Gorillas" were born.

They were recruited from penitentiaries all over the United States. Killers, con men, safecrackers, pickpockets, cat burglars.

"You name it, they've done it," Garrison said

to a reviewing board of officers once his band was formed. He grinned self-consciously. "You could say they're the cream of the underworld."

Of course, there had to be an inducement to make these criminals, these mavericks, these mugs, knuckle under to military discipline and risk their lives battling Nazis behind the enemy lines with the odds stacked against them. The deal was that if they worked with the military for the duration, then when the war was over their life sentences would be commuted. They would be free men again.

It had been rough in the beginning. Garrison felt as though he were a wild animal trainer in a cage with a bunch of wild jungle animals. He had been clawed a few times, but Lieutenant Garrison finally proved to them that he was tougher, rougher, and more determined than they were. He had whipped them into a fighting unit second to none in the world. Garrison's Gorillas performed a series of spectacular missions inside occupied Europe, inside the heart of Germany itself. There was one rumor that Adolf Hitler had regular nightmares of being captured by Garrison's band of outlaws.

It was true they were more outlaws than sol- diers—with a touch of Robin Hood's Merry Men and the Keystone Kops thrown in!

Craig Garrison was rightly proud of them. Winging across the English Channel in the dark of a foggy night in a B-17 bomber, he studied the faces of the crew he had picked for this particular mission.

The Chief, a huge, dark bear of a man, was a pure-blooded Indian. Hidden under his sweater he wore a special leather sheath that held a wicked knife with a blade almost a foot long. The Chief could stick a fly to the wall at a distance of thirty feet with that knife. His muscular fingers were busy braiding the ends of a leather thong garrote, another of his favored weapons.

Goniff, Casino, and the Actor were sitting on

the deck of the cabin with their legs folded under them, playing poker by the light of a hooded electric lantern.

Goniff was a slender, fair-haired man with foxy eyes and nervous, quicksilver movements. The warden of the prison where Garrison had found him said of Goniff: "He's the best pickpocket and cardsharp in the business." Goniff's quick, talented fingers and sharp mind had proved invaluable to the outfit.

Casino had been the most wanted cat burglar in the Middle West before the law put him away for life. He was a dark, stocky, angry-looking man with a beard like a wire brush. His specialty was "breaking and entering," as the law put it. Casino was Garrison's demolition expert.

The Actor really looked like a movie star— tall, dark, and handsome—and he was more talented than a lot of screen idols. The Actor had played so many different roles in his life that it was difficult to figure out who he really was!

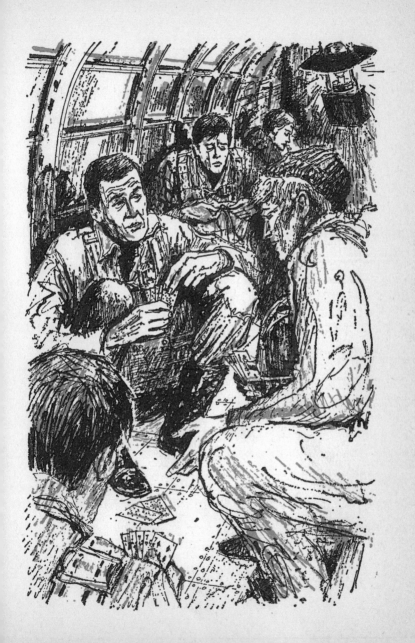

As a con man in the States he had bilked thousands of dollars out of gullible investors playing various roles—bank presidents, oil tycoons, English noblemen, and society playboys, among others. He could have fooled Hitler himself in the role of a German general.

Garrison looked over at the newest addition to their little group, who was snoozing in a corner of the cabin. "Casey—the Man With a Thousand Faces," as he was billed on "Wanted" posters across the United States before he joined up with the Gorillas. Casey was a small-boned, supple man with small features, exceptionally smooth skin for a man, and large green eyes. On first meeting, Casino had called him "pretty boy," and the next thing he knew, he was flat on his back with a numb jaw. It turned out that Casey had won the lightweight championship of the Golden Gloves a few years before the war.

Casey was a master impersonator and could pass himself off as any man—or woman—he had a clear photograph of. The high spot of his criminal career was when he lifted an emerald necklace from Tiffany's, the swank New York jewelers, posing as a prominent socialite.

Garrison was certain Casey was going to be a big asset to the team on this job.

And a tough job it was—one that the men were not at all enthusiastic about. Secretly Craig Garrison shared their worries. He had no ready answer when Casino tossed in his cards and muttered, "Finding this Kropotkin character is going to be worse than finding that proverbial needle in the haystack. He could be anywhere in Europe, and we don't even know what the guy looks like. Looks to me like the brass is really trying to get us bumped off this time, boss."

Casino winked at Goniff and the Actor. "What do you guys think?"

Garrison didn't go for the bait as he would have done when the outfit was first formed. In the early days he had cracked a few heads to enforce discipline. Now he let them shoot off their mouths as much as they wished. Let them blow off steam. Besides, he had learned, curiously, that he could often profit by listening to their idle, outspoken conversations. The criminal brain had a kind of raw, instinctive intelligence that he himself lacked—an animal cunning that did not always follow the average man's logical reasoning. It produced some interesting results.

"The way I see it," Goniff was saying, "this Kropotkin has been dodging the Nazis for almost two years. Right?"

"So?" Casino said.

"So it's not so different from running from the cops, is it?"

"Good point, Goniff," the Actor said in his rich voice.

Garrison's ears perked up but he said nothing to interrupt the discussion.

"Okay," said Goniff, "think about when you was on the lam—the longest stretch you was able to stay out of stir. How did you beat the cops at the game?"

Casey was awake now and he spoke up. "I got one that will really flip you guys. Once when the heat was on me real bad, I rented a room right across the street from a precinct house. Right under their noses. They even had my picture in the vestibule."

The Actor laughed. "A gem! Bright lad!"

"That's the point I was making." Goniff tapped his fingers on Garrison's knee. "When you're on the lam you try to pick a hideout that would be the last place they'd ever think of looking for you."

Garrison was excited. "What you're saying is that Emile Kropotkin may be holed up close to that Gestapo stronghold where they have his brother imprisoned?"

"Sure thing," Casino agreed. "Anyway, it's as good a place to start looking as any other."

Garrison spread out a silk scarf on the deck.

On it was imprinted a detailed map of occupied Europe. With a finger he indicated a spot near the Rhine River by the Franco-German border.

"Our checkpoint is Strasbourg. The underground will be expecting us to drop in tonight."

Casino slapped his parachute. "*Da!* Drop in! The warden's making jokes again."

"Button your lip, Casino," Garrison said, unsmiling. "This is a briefing." With his fingers he measured the distance between Strasbourg and Prague on the map. "We'll have to cross the southern part of Germany right here."

"Just what I always wanted to see," Goniff said gloomily. "The Black Forest in the springtime."

The Actor cuffed him on the back of the head. "You heard the warden. This is a briefing."

All the men laughed and Garrison felt his face reddening. The one way they could always get him riled up was to refer to him as "the warden."

"There's a lot of wooded country in southern

Germany. It will provide us with good cover," he told them.

A red light flashed on over the door leading to the cockpit, and a buzzer sounded.

"This is it, men," Lieutenant Garrison said as he stood up. "Prepare to bail out."

They lined up in single file at the open door and hooked up their chute cords to the trip wire overhead.

All during the flight the Chief had remained as silent as a cigar-store Indian. He had been known to go days without uttering a word to anyone except to grunt and nod his head. But when he did speak, Garrison had discovered, he usually had something keen and vital to say.

Just before he leaped out into the cold, starless night, the Chief turned to Garrison and asked, "If we find this Kropotkin—what do we do with him?"

It was the one question Garrison had been hoping none of his Gorillas would think to ask, because he knew that they weren't going to like the answer one little bit.

"Let's find him first," he mumbled and shoved the big Indian out the door.

4.

AMBUSH

It was a still night and the air drop was perfect. They fell into the woods on the outskirts of the city, screened by the heavy mist that often hung over the Rhine River country. Upon landing, each man stripped off his heavy flight coveralls and buried them along with his parachute. The rendezvous point with the French underground was at a nearby clearing.

Their contact, a thin man wearing a ragged sweater and cap, was sitting on a log, smoking a cigarette and staring into the dark.

"You're right on time," he said after they had exchanged passwords.

"Are there any Germans close by?" Garrison asked in perfect French. Both Garrison and the Actor spoke French and German fluently. The other Gorillas had been carefully and skillfully tutored in key phrases in both languages, so that they could pass a brief, casual encounter with any Nazi soldiers they might run into.

"Just a few roving patrols," the Frenchman replied. "It's been quiet tonight."

He examined the costumes worn by Lieutenant Garrison and his band. They were dressed like German peasants. Or they could just as readily pose as French farmers. The natives of the district on both sides of the Rhine, French and German, wore simple, nondescript clothing.

"My orders are to get you started properly in whatever direction you choose to go," he said. "And where will it be?"

Garrison pointed to the east. "We're going to Prague. We have good reason to believe Emile Kropotkin may be hiding right under the noses of the Gestapo."

"An interesting notion," the Frenchman said. "As you know, the maquis and the underground in all of the occupied countries have been working hand in hand with the Allies to keep him from falling into German hands. My personal opinion is that Emile Kropotkin is dead and buried. Otherwise we would have received some hint of his whereabouts after all these months."

Garrison rubbed his lean jaw and frowned. "There's always that possibility, of course."

"In which case we're on a wild-goose chase," Casino complained.

Garrison sighed. "Alive or dead, we have to find out for sure. All right, where do we go from here?"

The Frenchman took out a small black notebook and studied it by the light of a wooden

47

match. After leafing through a few pages, he looked up.

"There's a freight at Baden-Baden scheduled to leave for the Eastern Front tomorrow morning at dawn. It's carrying tanks and cannon and should be routed through Prague."

"How far is Baden-Baden from here?"

"Twenty miles or so."

Garrison nodded grimly. "We've got to be on that train when it leaves."

"Twenty miles is a long walk," said the Actor.

"You can't risk motor transportation," the Frenchman said. "Not six men."

Garrison thought a moment. "Those German patrols you mentioned—are they on foot?"

"No, they ride bicycles. Eight-man squads, and they patrol a ten-mile stretch of road."

"Fine," Garrison said. "Suppose you take us to the closest road where we'll be apt to run into one of these patrols."

The Frenchman's eyes lit up. "Ah, yes! I see

what you have in mind. Can we be of service? I can support you with ten men. They are standing on alert back at headquarters."

"Thanks, but I think we can handle it by ourselves," Garrison told him. "Anyway, in case something goes wrong and we walk into a trap, it's best that your people stay clear. The underground can't afford to lose a single man needlessly. The invasion of Europe by the Allies is right around the corner, and your help will be vital to its success."

"I understand. . . ." The Frenchman studied them silently for a moment. "Your name is famous in our organization, Lieutenant Garrison. The Gestapo would love to get its hands on you. How is it your leaders are willing to risk losing such valuable people as Garrison's Gorillas on such an unimportant mission? This Emile Kropotkin, he is just one little man. A scientist." He shrugged his shoulders.

Garrison turned on a tight smile and put a hand

on the man's shoulder. "My friend," he said quietly, "if the Germans get their hands on Emile Kropotkin before we find him, he might just turn out to be the most important and biggest man in the world! Now lead on. We only have about six hours left before daylight."

It was going to be a long night, thought Sgt. Fritz Kunstler of the *Wehrmacht* military police as he pedaled his bike at the head of his column along the dark road. The night was chill and damp, and they would not be relieved until 4:00 A.M. And the patrol was all so pointless. In three months since he had been assigned to the post, Kunstler and his men had come up against nothing more dangerous than idle drunks or a poor frightened farmer scurrying home after curfew. Fritz Kunstler was restless for some real action.

He did not realize it, but it was waiting for him right around the next bend in the road.

As the cyclists rounded the turn, they saw three figures apparently fighting in the middle of the road about a hundred feet ahead. Kunstler flicked on the electric lamp on his handlebars, illuminating three rough-looking men in peasant dress. Two of them seemed to be attacking the third man, who was knocked to the ground as the German soldiers approached. When Kunstler shouted to them, the two fled in opposite directions into the woods at the sides of the road, leaving the other man sprawled out motionless in the dust.

"Halt!" the sergeant screamed, fumbling for the Luger pistol holstered at his side. By the time he had it out and his men had scrambled off their bikes and unslung their carbines off their shoulders, the two fleeing men were lost in the thick trees.

Kunstler snapped out orders. "Corporal Schultz, take two men and follow that one!" He pointed to one side of the road. "Keller, you take two men and go after the other one. . . . Katz, you come with me. Looks like they may have killed this fellow."

He put his pistol back into its holster and approached the man who was lying still on his back in the middle of the road. They kneeled down, one on each side of him, and the sergeant shined a torch into the face of Craig Garrison.

Garrison opened his eyes slowly. Sergeant Kunstler had a premonition. He felt as though he was staring into the barrels of twin pistols as he gazed into Garrison's hard eyes.

"Are you all right?" he asked the stranger.

There was no reply.

"What happened?" Kunstler tried again. "What is this all about?"

"This!" Garrison snapped. His arms came up behind the Germans' backs, one on each side of him, and his hands closed like vises on the backs of their necks. With a mighty effort, he crashed their heads together. Without a murmur, the

Nazi soldiers crumpled in the road.

In the woods on one side of the road, Corporal Schultz led his men charging among the trees, with his carbine held at port arms. As they passed by a thick oak, in single file, neither Schultz nor the man in back of him saw the thin leather thong flash out to wrap snakelike around the throat of the last man in line. The terrified German had a brief glimpse of a large face with shining white teeth inches from his own. Strangely, it reminded him of a savage face that had haunted his dreams after seeing an American-made movie about a battle between cowboys and Indians. Then he blacked out.

Up ahead, flattened against the bole of another tree, Casino heard the Germans crashing toward him. He lifted his right hand, fingers held stiff and close together, poised high in the air like an ax blade.

He let the first one pass, then poleaxed the second with a deadly karate chop behind the ear.

The German went down in the brush, two hundred pounds of dead weight. As he fell, his outstretched hands hit the backs of Corporal Schultz's heels, almost tripping him.

He caught his balance and whirled around, shouting angrily, *"Dummkopf!"*

His cry choked in his throat as he saw the dark, huddled form on the ground. Standing a few feet farther back was Casino. In the darkness, the confused corporal mistook him for the third German soldier.

"Werner's passed out," he said in a puzzled voice. He unsnapped a flashlight from his belt and turned it on the soldier on the ground.

The little circle of light just took in Casino's legs from the knees down. It took the corporal a moment to realize that these legs and feet were not in *Wehrmacht* combat boots. With a little gasp, he flicked the light up into Casino's dark, sardonic face.

"Ach! Himmel!" he shouted and swung up

the muzzle of his carbine—just as Goniff stepped up behind him and dispatched him with one swipe of a thick tree branch.

On the other side of the road the Actor and Casey were having a little more trouble with Corporal Keller and his two charges. Casey had cleanly picked off the third man in line as the Germans ran past his ambush point.

The Actor brought the second man down with a karate chop, but the punch was not clean, and it only stunned the German. He fell to his knees, moaning so loudly that the corporal heard him and turned back. The beam of his flashlight pinned the Actor to a tree. The Actor ducked under the light and launched a flying tackle at Keller. The muzzle flash of the carbine singed the back of his neck as he crashed against the German's legs. The corporal sprawled out on his back, and the Actor swatted the carbine out of his hands. He climbed on top of Keller and drove a knee into his belly. The air whooshed out of the man's lungs, leaving him paralyzed. The Actor chopped him backhanded on the Adam's apple, completing the job.

At the same time, the stunned German, recovering quickly, staggered to his knees and aimed his carbine at the Actor's back. Casey came running up fast to join the fight, but he was still fifteen feet away as the soldier's finger closed on the trigger.

Casey felt something strange whizzing inches away from his right ear. He was astonished to see the German drop the carbine and fall forward on his face with a groan. The Actor picked up one of the German flashlights and turned it on the fallen man. He had been stabbed. The knife had a familiar, elaborately carved ivory handle designed like a small totem pole.

"The Chief!" Casey and the Actor chorused.

The big Indian seemed to materialize magically out of the night without a sound. His face was impassive.

"Where the devil did you come from?" Casey asked.

The Chief's mouth turned up slightly at the corners, in an expression that was the closest he ever came to smiling.

"General Custer didn't call the U. S. Indians 'the ghosts' for nothing, Mac!" he grunted. He got his knife back and returned to the road.

As they regrouped in the road, the Frenchman from the underground came up with two of his friends.

"We were watching to see how you came out," he told Garrison.

Garrison grinned at the sight of the grenades on their belts and the submachine guns slung over their shoulders.

"You decided we needed reserves anyway?" he asked jokingly.

The Frenchman shrugged. "Our apologies, Lieutenant. It was foolish of us. After all—" he put one hand on Garrison's shoulder and the other on Casino's shoulder—"you are Garrison's Gorillas."

The Americans laughed, except for the Chief.

"Let's round up those bikes, men," Garrison snapped. "And get the uniforms off those Germans. On the double!"

"Hut!" Casino and Goniff snapped to attention and saluted.

Garrison aimed a playful kick at them, but they scurried away.

"What about the Germans?" the Frenchman wanted to know as Garrison and the others were putting on the *Wehrmacht* uniforms. "All of them are still alive. Two are in bad shape, though. The one who was knifed is the worst."

Garrison's face was stony. "I'll leave it up to the underground. If you feel they can be of any use to you alive, take them prisoner. If not. . . ." He left the thought unfinished.

Nobody ever claimed that war was fun and games, he thought with a trace of bitterness. Men were wounded. Men died. It was a brutal, dirty business. You had to be hard as nails to stay alive.

"All right, men," he said quietly. "Get on those bikes and let's move out."

They mounted and rode off, waving to the Frenchmen in the road behind them.

They looked as natural as any other German mounted patrol. Garrison hoped so, at least. He was a little worried about the Chief's bronzed complexion and dark hair and piercing black eyes. But he had seen many dark, swarthy Germans from the southland who, with a deep suntan, did not look too unlike the big Indian.

They rode swiftly toward Baden-Baden.

5.

JOURNEY
WITH TIGERS

ONCE THEY PASSED another bicycle patrol riding in the opposite direction. Garrison exchanged a cheerful greeting with the squad's leader in German as both groups braked to a halt at the side of the road.

"Aren't you off your own beat, Sergeant?" the German inquired curiously.

"Our CO just took us off our regular patrol," Garrison lied easily. "Told us to report to the railyards in Baden-Baden for special duty. I don't know what it's all about either."

He cast a quick look around at his Gorillas in the blue light of dawn. They sat astride their bikes, looking very casual, but he observed that their hands rested lightly on their weapons. The Chief had one hand inside his tunic. Garrison guessed his fingers were caressing the ivory handle of his knife.

"Well, good luck." The German patrol leader touched the peak of his cap and rode on.

On the outskirts of the city, they pedaled up boldly to a sentry box at an intersection. Garrison asked the Nazi MP how to get to the main rail-yards.

"About one mile, this way." The German pointed down the road to their left.

Not long after that they were approaching the high steel fence topped with barbed wire that ran around the perimeter of the railyards. Three helmeted guards armed with submachine guns and one officer, a captain, were on duty there.

Garrison saluted the captain, a thin hawk-faced man who was pacing up and down with jerky mechanical steps, his back stiff as a poker.

"The adjutant's office told us to report to the dispatch office for special guard duty," Garrison said.

For a reason that was not at once clear to Garrison, the German captain became suddenly infuriated.

"You men, all of you! Get off those bicycles!" he roared, his face turning crimson. "Line up before me at attention!"

Badly shaken, the Gorillas laid down their bikes and obeyed. Garrison was tense. Was it possible that the Germans were on to their game? It couldn't be! Still, his muscles were braced to go into action at the first indication of real danger.

The German officer strutted up and down in front of them, glowering. He stopped in front of Garrison.

"Let me see your identification tags!" he

snapped. "Quickly now! Do not waste my time!"

Craig Garrison thanked the good luck that had prompted him to borrow the unconscious sergeant's dog tags. He opened his collar and slipped a finger under the thin chain on which the tags were suspended inside his shirt. As he exposed the metal tags he stole a quick look at the name and serial number stamped on them. The number had eight digits, and he had only an instant to glance at it.

The captain cupped them in one hand and squinted at them. "Name?" he snapped.

"Staff-Sergeant Fritz Kunstler," Garrison replied promptly.

"Serial number?"

Garrison hesitated and inhaled deeply. *Here goes!* he thought. "Three-two-seven-one-eight-two-nine-two!" he rattled it off.

The captain dropped the tags and they jangled against Garrison's chest on the chain. He clasped his hands behind his back and scowled at Garrison.

"How did you ever make the grade of sergeant when you are so ignorant of proper military rules?" he asked. "Don't you know it is improper to salute a superior officer while you are mounted on a bicycle?"

"I apologize, *Herr* Captain," Garrison said. "I don't know where my mind is. I guess I'm just tired, sir. We've already pulled one tour of duty, and now they put us on this one for another six hours."

"No matter. I think I just may make an example of you, Sergeant. Who is your commanding officer, and where is his headquarters?"

Garrison's voice box was paralyzed. It looked as if they were going to have to fight their way out of this fix. His fingers crept up his thigh toward the Luger pistol holstered to his right hip.

Just then a telephone inside the sentry box at one side of the gate began to ring urgently.

"It's for you, sir," a voice inside the hut called out. "Colonel Strang on the line."

Muttering, the captain did an about-face and stalked into the sentry box. One of the guards, a sergeant with a sympathetic face, came up to Garrison and whispered.

"Get on your bikes and get going," he said. "We call him Captain Rat. One of these days he's going to get a bullet in his back." He grinned. "A German bullet!"

Garrison grinned and relaxed. They had 'em in every army, he guessed. "Thanks," he said to the sergeant.

He and the Gorillas scrambled for their bikes and rode through the gate toward the sidings about a quarter of a mile farther on.

Casino and the Actor pulled up even with Garrison's bike. "Close shave, warden," Casino said.

"Nice job of acting. I couldn't have done better myself," the Actor laughed. "Sergeant Kunstler! I thought he had you on the serial number, though. Whew!"

Garrison nodded grimly. "That long freight to the left side—it must be the one." Seven flatcars near the end of the train carried Tiger tanks, strapped down and covered with tarpaulins. There was a locomotive at each end of the big freight train. A whistle hooted mournfully on the rear engine. Up front the other locomotive answered with its whistle. Steam jetted out of the brake lines of the cars.

"They're just about ready to pull out," Garrison said.

He led his group down the far side of the freight train where another line of cars on an adjacent track shielded their movements from view.

"We'd better ditch these bikes first thing," Garrison suggested. "In one of these empty cars." He indicated the boxcars on the other track, and it was quickly accomplished.

"Now follow me and act like you really belong here," Garrison instructed them. They walked along the long line of trains, testing the ropes and wires that tied down the heavy tanks on the flat-cars and inspecting the big padlocks that sealed the closed freight cars.

On the other side of the train they heard march-ing feet approaching. Garrison peered between two cars and saw a formation of soldiers heading in their direction. They were dressed warmly in heavy overcoats, with woolen caps underneath their helmets. Their rifles were slung across their backs. They were the train guards, outfitted for the long, windy trip across Germany while perched on top of the cars.

Garrison continued down the line of cars until he found what he was looking for—a flatcar car-rying four tanks, with good cover on both sides: the empty cars on one side, a tall pyramid of pack-ing cases on the other side.

"Okay, boys, up we go." He vaulted onto the flatcar and cut the lines that held down the tar-paulin that covered the turret of the nearest tank. "Casino, you and Goniff get inside this baby."

"You mean we're gonna stay in this tin can all the way to Prague?" Goniff protested. "I'll starve to death!"

"Don't be a fool," Garrison snapped. "It can't be more than a twelve-hour trip. These trains have special priority. Anyway, there are probably canned emergency rations already tucked away somewhere inside the tank if you get hungry."

Casino and Goniff disappeared inside the turret and closed the hatch. Garrison pulled the tarp over it again loosely, fastening the broken ends of the lines with slipknots which could be easily unraveled by a strong tug on the tarp.

Then they hurried along to the next tank, and the Chief and Casey piled into the turret.

Garrison and the Actor climbed into the third tank on the flatcar. Before he lowered the turret, Garrison draped the tarp over it loosely and drew his head inside. There was no way to rig the cut lines this time. He crossed his fingers and hoped the German guards wouldn't notice.

He and the Actor settled down in seats designed for the tank's crewmen. It was pitch-dark. Garrison fumbled blindly on the dashboard and control panel, looking for the switch that operated the front observation vents. He found it at last, and the armor flaps that covered the vents slid up. But he had forgotten about the tarp. Still no light. He took out his knife and with the razor-sharp blade slit the heavy canvas where it covered the viewing port. Then he did the same on the Actor's side. Two thin slivers of daylight were now visible. Gradually their eyes became accustomed to the dim interior of the steel monster.

The whistles sounded again, the train lurched, there was a hissing of steam as the brakes were released, and they were off, rumbling in the direction of Prague.

Garrison opened the slit in the tarp a little with his fingers and peered out. On the tank ahead of them, at the front of the flatcar, a stout soldier was seated on top of the turret, basking in

71

the early-morning sun. His back was to them. After a while another guard appeared on top of the narrow walk of the next boxcar and shouted down to the stout German.

"Well, we're off, Hans."

"Yes," the other answered. "I'm thankful it isn't raining, anyway."

The guard on the catwalk laughed grimly. "Enjoy it while you can. Wait until we get into Russia." He hugged himself with his arms and shivered. "Brrrr!"

They were on the outskirts of the city now, picking up speed. The man on the boxcar nodded. "I'd better get back to the front of the car now. Once we really get moving, it's not so much fun to walk along the top of one of these cars." He grinned. "You're lucky to be on a flatcar."

"How so?"

"Last trip I had a tank car. Once we clear Stuttgart, we don't stop again for another six hours. You can climb into one of those Tigers and have a nice snooze for yourself."

The fat guard laughed. "I never thought of that. Thanks for the idea."

A cold finger ran down Garrison's spine. The Actor read his thoughts. "Suppose Jerry picks this tank to sack out in?"

Garrison didn't answer. He kept hearing the loose tarpaulin flapping in the wind. If the German decided to nap in one of the tanks, this was the logical one to choose. The tarp was already partially off.

An hour and a half later they ground to a clattering stop. There was the sound of much activity outside. Garrison peered out through the slit in the tarp and saw they were in a teeming railroad yard. The guard was standing up on the side of the car now, feet spread wide, hands behind his back. He came to attention and saluted as a sergeant and an officer came down the line to make a brief inspection.

The officer saw the loose tarp on the tank

73

Garrison and the Actor were in. "Get that tarpaulin tied down at once, soldier!" he ordered.

"Yes, sir!" the guard said, saluting again. He came over to the big Tiger tank and fussed with the tarp and the cut lines. He made a big show of it, but he tied a very simple, loose knot. As soon as they were on their way again, he was going to take his good friend's advice and have a fine snooze for himself!

6.

END OF THE LINE

Soon after the train began to roll again, Garrison heard the heavy boots clomping on the steel deck of the Tiger tank as the guard climbed aboard. He shut the observation vents and pulled the Actor to the very rear of the dark, cramped space. They flattened themselves against the metal sides of the tank and held their breath.

The turret swung open and daylight streamed into the tank. A pair of heavy legs and clumsy boots slowly descended through the hole. The stout German was puffing from exertion. His hips came through, then his stomach and chest. Finally he dropped with a thud to the floor plates.

The guard's eyes were unaccustomed to the dimness after coming out of the bright sunlight. He blinked to clear his vision. Gradually forms and shapes became visible. He almost smiled. His mind must be playing tricks with him. Human faces! Imagine!

The smile died abruptly as Garrison and the Actor moved toward him. He gave a soft outcry before an iron fist crashed into his soft belly. He grabbed his middle and doubled over. Garrison sliced the edge of his hand down hard on the thick neck, and the guard sank into deep unconsciousness. They removed his overcoat, gloves, wool cap, and helmet. Then they tied him up and climbed out of the tank. The train was speeding through desolate forest land, the wind whistling past their ears.

Garrison sent the Actor back to rouse the

other Gorillas out of the tanks farther back on the flatcar. He put on the German's cap, helmet, gloves, and overcoat. The coat was several sizes too large, but it would have to do. He slung the guard's rifle over his shoulder.

His men gathered around him. "Here's the pitch," Garrison told them. "I'll take the guard's place up front on the first tank. With any luck we'll make it all the way to the outskirts of Prague."

"How about when the train crosses the border?" Casey wondered. "There's bound to be a check-point at the Czech border."

"What border?" Casino sneered. "The Nazis own everything on the continent."

Garrison frowned. "No matter, they make sure they keep the people in the occupied countries very well penned up. Czechoslovakia is one big prison camp. Casey's right. We may run into trouble at the border. In any case, we'll have to be ready for it. Actor, you come up front with me

77

and get in the first tank. The rest of you deploy in the other tanks. Get rid of the tarps altogether now. If we get in any tight spots, you can shoot through the front vents."

Casino patted the long snout of one of the tank's cannon. "Too bad we ain't got any ammo for these babies."

An inspiration hit Garrison. "You're so right, Casino! I almost didn't think of it!"

"Huh?" Casino's jaw dropped.

"The tanks! There must be a quarter of a tank of fuel in each one. Just think about it! We have our own little armored division right here on this flatcar!"

Goniff let out a long, low whistle. "Cripes! I never thought of that! Bring on the whole German army!"

They worked energetically, stripping the tanks for action, cutting the lines and wires that tied them down.

"Let's just hope we don't go around any sharp

curves," the Actor said as he let himself down into the first tank on the car while Garrison took up the guard's post on the turret. The Chief and Casey manned the one behind it, and Goniff and Casino took the third tank. There was no longer any need for strict precautions now that the German guard was taken care of. They spent the next hour reading the operating manual that was chained to the dashboard above the driver's seat. The interior lights were all ablaze.

Garrison's Gorillas had undergone intensive instruction back in England in the use of every weapon in the Nazi arsenal. It took little effort and time to refresh their memories about the Tiger tank, the terrible German Mark VI.

Passing through a stretch of mountains, the train slowed almost to a crawl. The German sentry on the boxcar ahead made his way back on the catwalk.

"Hello!" he shouted to Garrison in a surprised voice. "What happened to Hans?"

"He took sick," Garrison lied. "I was put on at Stuttgart."

The German, a dark, husky fellow with keen eyes, frowned. "That's funny. I spoke to him a little while before we got to Stuttgart. He was fine then."

Garrison shrugged. "Something he ate, no doubt."

The German said nothing. His sharp eyes were traveling over the flatcar, taking in the broken lines on the first three tanks, the missing tarpaulins. Only an idiot would not be suspicious! Garrison took a desperate gamble.

"You know something," he said to the German, with a nervous glance across his shoulder. "There is a very peculiar thing about this car. I noticed it when I got on at Stuttgart."

"What is it?" the man demanded guardedly.

"I'll come up there and tell you," Garrison said. "I don't like this shouting." He cleared his throat loudly. "Laryngitis."

"Come ahead," the German said. His face was expressionless.

Garrison walked to the front of the flatcar and stepped across onto the apron of the boxcar. A metal ladder went straight up the back wall of the car. The train began to pick up speed again as he climbed.

His head cleared the top of the car. His eyes widened in shock. He was staring into the muzzle of the German's Mauser rifle.

"All right, you! No tricks!" the guard snapped. "Get up here!"

Garrison felt like a dunce. He had come up here to outfox the German, only to be outfoxed himself. He crawled up on the narrow walk that ran down the center of the car's roof and stood up.

"Let the rifle slip off your shoulder," the German ordered. His rifle was pointed at Garrison's chest, and his trigger finger was tense in the trigger guard.

81

Garrison let the rifle slide to the roof. The German moved toward him. "Hands up high. That's it." He kicked the rifle and it went sailing into empty space, clattering in the bluestones along the track's right-of-way.

With the gun held on Garrison with one hand, the guard fumbled inside his heavy coat with the other hand for a pair of handcuffs. It was a fatal error! On top of a swaying boxcar, it was difficult to hold a rifle steady with two hands. But with the stock wedged under his armpit and only one hand to balance it, the German lost all control of the long rifle barrel. The muzzle swung back and forth in a wide arc. Timing his move perfectly, Garrison sprang at his captor with the fierce swiftness of a tiger.

The German fired, but the shot was wide of its mark by two feet. Then Garrison was on him. He shoved the barrel aside with his left hand and chopped a short right to the German's heavy jaw. The guard was tougher than most. His head snapped back and he grunted in pain, but he did not go down. He tried to kick Garrison, but the American blocked the boot with his hand. He jerked the leg up as hard as he could and the German landed on his back. The rifle crashed to the car roof and went skating over to the edge. Then the German made his second mistake. He went scrambling on all fours after his rifle. And then, as the guard squatted at the edge of the boxcar's roof on hands and knees, Garrison leaped up behind him. Before the German could whirl and bring up the rifle, Garrison, a football star in his college days, delivered the punt of his whole lifetime—squarely on the man's broad, upturned seat.

With a yowl of surprise and terror, the soldier went sailing out into space. The last sight Garrison had of him was as he went rolling through the bushes like a rubber ball going down a steep hillside.

The Czech border was only minutes away now.

The border checkpoint was heavily guarded, and the tracks were illuminated by glaring floodlights over a distance of several hundred feet. German officers with flashlights and enlisted men armed with submachine guns and automatic rifles went down the line from the locomotive up front, checking each of the cars carefully.

Garrison alerted his Gorillas for action, then took his place at the front of the flatcar, standing at parade rest. His heart beat faster as the inspection party reached the boxcar directly ahead.

A shout went up. "The guard is not here."

After excited discussion among the officers, the group moved back to where Garrison was. He came to attention and saluted.

"Do you know anything about the guard on the next car?" a captain asked him.

"Yes, sir," Garrison said. "I think he went over the hill, sir. He was drinking rather heavily on the way from Baden-Baden. I'd say he was drunk. He complained about the army and going

84

to the Eastern front. About five miles back, he said he wasn't going no matter what happened to him. He jumped off." Garrison shrugged his shoulders.

The Nazi officers talked among themselves angrily for several minutes. Then the captain turned back to Garrison.

"All right, soldier. You've done well to tell us about this swine. I promise you, he won't get far."

"I hope not, sir," Garrison said, trying not to smile. "One thing I can't stand is a traitor!"

"Good man." The captain returned his salute and started to move on.

Just then, one of the German soldiers, who had been running a powerful flashlight over the tanks on the flatcar, shouted.

"Three of these Mark Sixes have been cut loose. Their tarpaulins have been ripped off as well."

A heavyset sergeant with the flat, broken face of a prizefighter scowled at Garrison and shined a light in his face.

"Wait a minute!" he growled. "You're not

Hans Mahler." He took out a duty roster and showed it to the captain. "I thought something queer was going on here. Sir, this man is an impostor. I'm sure of it!"

Garrison didn't wait to hear any more. He reached the tank in one leap. Another leap took him up to the turret, and he dove through the opening headfirst as a volley of shots clanged against the steel sides of the Tiger tank. He pulled the turret shut and yelled to the Actor.

"Let's get rolling!"

In back of them, the other Gorillas had got the message. He heard the whine and roar of their powerful engines coming to life. Their exhausts shot smoke and sparks.

Garrison grabbed the microphone of the tank's communication radio. He twirled the dial, seeking the proper frequency.

"Do you read me? . . . Do you read me? . . . This is Garrison. . . . Do you read me?"

Distorted by the static, a voice finally answered,

"Roger, warden! I read you. This is Casino."

Right on top of it, Casey's voice came in: "Casey here, Lieutenant. What do we do now?"

"Half right turn," Garrison said. "We'll go off the car on the left side. It looks softer over there. Just follow me."

He swiveled his Tiger so that the nose was pointing straight at the German soldiers grouped on the ground next to the car. Through the observation slits he could see them hopping around excitedly and pouring machine-gun and rifle fire at the three tanks. The slugs bounced off the steel plating like raindrops bursting against a windowpane. Garrison advanced the throttle, threw in the clutch, and the gigantic steel monster went lurching forward. It teetered an instant on the edge of the car, swinging back and forth like a pendulum, then the nose dipped down and off she went. The Germans scattered in all directions.

The shock of landing rattled Garrison's teeth, and if it had not been for their seat belts, he and the Actor would have been shaken inside the cabin like a pair of dice. The big, tough tank shuddered, but that was all. It had been built to withstand far greater punishment on the battlefield.

Garrison gave it the gun, and they went rumbling past the buildings at the checkpoint in majestic order, one, two, three in a row. From all sides the Germans were pelting them with fire. But none of the weapons at the checkpoint were of a caliber to stop a Tiger tank. There were few weapons, even in England, that could knock out a Mark VI, Garrison reflected.

In minutes they had left the checkpoint and the Nazis far behind and were rolling along a good dirt road into the Czechoslovakian countryside.

When they had covered ten miles Garrison led them off the road and down a dark, wooded lane with a thick arch of tree branches overhead. Deep in the woods, he stopped the tank and opened the

turret. He and the Actor climbed out and assembled with the others.

"We can't risk going any farther in these tanks," he told them. "By now they'll have alerted headquarters that there are three runaway Tigers in the district. Every available tank destroyer outfit will be after us. The *Luftwaffe,* too. . . . Listen!" He pointed upward.

A low-flying plane zoomed over the trees above them. There were other planes in the sky.

"They've got the spotters looking for us already," Garrison said. "They won't find us here— not from the air, at least. But we'd better take off before the area is swarming with soldiers."

He removed the back from his wristwatch, then the crystal, which converted into a magnifying lens. By the glow of a shielded flashlight he studied the tiny notations etched into the inside cover of the watch. They recorded the identity and location of every underground contact currently operating in Nazi-occupied Europe.

"I guess Balzer is the man we want to find," he said. He put the watch back together again.

On his scarf map he plotted their position at present. "Let's see, Balzer is about fifteen miles to the northeast of here, give or take a mile."

"It should be fun getting there," the Actor commented. "Especially since this area is swarming with German soldiers, all looking for us."

Garrison grinned. "It will be easier than you think. We look like German soldiers, don't we?" He indicated their uniforms. "And our carbines are still in the tanks. So all we have to do is pretend that *we're* looking for us, too!"

7.

A LABORATORY PRISON

THEY FOUND Balzer without once being challenged by the numerous German patrols they met on the way. He lived in a small broken-down hut off a cow path in the deep woods. As they approached, he was chopping firewood on a tree stump at one side of the hut. A large man with curly black hair and a nose like an eagle, he straightened up and leaned on his ax, watching them with suspicion and undisguised hatred. All night long, squads of Nazi soldiers had been

THE FEAR FORMULA

pounding on his door and asking him about the "traitorous spies" who were loose in the vicinity. He had hardly had any sleep at all, and at dawn he had gone outside to work off his anger with the ax.

"Balzer?" Garrison inquired.

"That's what they call me," he answered guardedly. "What's wrong?"

Garrison gave him the underground's password. "Rain from the west. It looks like rain from the west."

Balzer shrugged and went back to his woodcutting. "No, the wind from the east will blow the storm clouds away," he said.

"Lightning," Garrison said.

"Thunder." The unfriendly peasant face broke out in a grin, and he dropped the ax and held out his hand to Garrison. His gaze passed over the Gorillas in their German uniforms.

"I might have guessed. Garrison's Gorillas," he said with pleasure. "Nobody else could give the

Germans such terrible nightmares as they have been having these past twelve hours."

"Where can we talk?" Garrison asked.

Balzer looked all about them very carefully. "I don't think we'll have to worry about the Nazi swine anymore today. They've been over this sector with a fine-tooth comb already. Come inside."

He led them into the hut. It was a shabby place with one big room and a small bedroom and pantry off to the back. He shoved the table in the center of the main room to one side and threw back a tattered rug. There was a trapdoor in the floor, so skillfully hidden that Garrison was not aware it was there until Balzer swung it open. He motioned for them to descend a ladder which led down into an underground chamber. When the lamps were lit, Garrison and his men were surprised to find themselves in an up-to-date radio communications center. Balzer was the commander of a thirty-man group of Czech patriots who had been battling the Nazi invaders since their country had been overrun. They blew up bridges, sabotaged German installations, and helped political prisoners and Allied prisoners escape to England or Switzerland.

"I am the last person the Nazis would ever suspect," Balzer explained. "They think I'm the ideal collaborator. I do blacksmith work for them. I cut their firewood. I lick their boots. They trust me completely."

"Even the Gestapo?" Garrison asked.

"I don't see much of the Gestapo," Balzer said. "They are too busy guarding the laboratory where Jules Kropotkin is held prisoner."

"How far is it from here?"

"About a mile up the road. Not the main highway—the dirt road that this path leads into."

"This lab you mentioned—it's heavily guarded, I suppose."

Balzer sighed. "Yes. You will see for yourself later on. If you are thinking of storming the laboratory directly, forget it. You'd need a battalion of soldiers."

"Then we must do it another way," Garrison said.

Balzer nodded gravely as he lit up his pipe. "Tell me, Lieutenant Garrison, what makes you believe that Emile Kropotkin is hiding in this vicinity?"

Garrison outlined their theory that Emile would reason that the last place the Gestapo would expect to find him was on their very doorstep.

"That is very interesting," the Czech said, puffing up a cloud of smoke. "Our people have had no more success than have the Germans in locating him. And we are his friends. Don't you think, Lieutenant, that if he was close by that he would find a way to let us know? After all, he is not running away from us."

Garrison shook his head. "Not necessarily true, Balzer. A frightened, hunted man sees danger in every direction. He doesn't trust anyone. Every occupied country has its traitors who sell out to the enemy."

"That is so," Balzer admitted. "But if Emile Kropotkin is here, where can he be? Our organization has a file on every man, woman, and child within a twenty-five mile radius. The identity of each one is verified beyond any doubt. A man like Emile Kropotkin could not hide himself from our agents for so many months."

"You may be right," Garrison admitted, "but we have to start looking somewhere, and this is it. . . . You say you are on good terms with the Germans at the lab. Have you been inside?"

"No, the security is too tight. They would not permit anyone inside the laboratory. . . ." He hesitated. "Well, no one except Kati, that is, and she doesn't count."

"Who is Kati?"

"A young woman who lives with an old crone near the lab. The old one is crippled, and the state put the girl there to take care of her. Something happened to the girl's head during a bombing raid. She has the mind of a small child. She does the laundry for the soldiers at the laboratory, and sometimes they permit her inside to sew on buttons and do other seamstress work for them."

"Can she be trusted?" Garrison asked. "You said she has the mind of a child."

Balzer smiled. "And who can keep a secret better than a child? For a child, it is a very serious business, keeping secrets. 'Cross your heart and hope to die.' Kati has done several small errands for the underground—delivering messages, things like that. It is an exciting game for her."

Garrison was still not convinced. This Kati might suddenly decide to play the same game for the Germans! After all, it seemed they treated her in a kindly way. But she was the only hope they had, and he had to take the chance.

"Tell me, Lieutenant," Balzer asked him, "if you are lucky enough to find Emile Kropotkin, what then?"

"That's what we've been trying to find out," the Actor said with a little smile. "What about it, warden? You can't avoid the question forever."

Garrison took a deep breath and braced himself for the storm he knew was coming.

"Yeah, wait just a minute!" Casino spoke up excitedly. "Why all this talk about the laboratory? What do we care if it's guarded or not? Our mission is to find Emile Kropotkin, and you don't think he's hiding in there, do you?"

"Finding Emile is only half the mission," Garrison gave it to them bluntly. "The other part of it is to rescue Jules Kropotkin and to get them both back safely into Allied hands."

"Oh, no!" The Gorillas closed in on him from all sides, all talking at once.

"You heard what the man said: It would take a battalion of soldiers to break into the place where they're holding Kropotkin!"

"It's a bum rap, Lieutenant! We didn't sign up with this outfit to commit suicide!"

"I should have stayed back in that nice peaceful jail," the Chief muttered.

"Then why didn't you?" Garrison snapped. "You men are soldiers, and I'm your commanding officer. Don't you ever forget it!"

"Sez who?" Casino shoved his jaw into Garrison's face.

Garrison's uppercut traveled such a short distance and so fast that Casino never saw it. It exploded on the point of his chin with the force of a grenade. He saw colored lights, and the next thing he knew he was sitting on the dirt floor with the room spinning around him. When the fog cleared, he looked up at Garrison. The other Gorillas were standing around looking very stiff and quiet.

"Get up and fall into ranks," Garrison snapped.

"Okay." Casino got up slowly and brushed himself off.

"*Okay?*" Garrison advanced toward him, his fists balling up.

100

"I mean, *yes, sir!*" Casino said hastily and stepped back into line alongside the Chief.

Suddenly Lieutenant Garrison grinned. "Now we understand each other. Right, you big apes?"

"Right," they said all together, their hard faces grinning back at him. In spite of their grumbling and complaining, there was not a man among them who would not have walked into hell itself —if Craig Garrison was leading the way.

He scolded them gently. "All of us have been in this outfit long enough to know better than to worry about the future. We have to live each day as it comes. Each minute. It isn't the Boy Scouts."

"That's the truth," Goniff said under his breath.

Garrison turned to Balzer. "Can you take us to see the laboratory?"

"At once," the Czech agreed. "But first you must get out of those uniforms." From a hamper in a corner he pulled out a variety of shirts, sweaters, and other clothing such as was worn by the natives of the region.

101

When they were dressed he took them through the thickest woods over a long, zigzagging course to a hill overlooking the place where Jules Kropotkin was being held prisoner.

The dwelling was a rambling chalet that had belonged to a government official before the war. The Germans had converted it into a fortress. The land had been cleared around the property, and two steel fences had been built to enclose the house, one inside of the other. Both had electrically charged high-tension wires running along their tops.

The guard detail was made up of fourteen Nazi soldiers that they could see—three at the outer gate, three at the inner gate, three patrols of two men each that roved around the perimeter of the outside fence, and a soldier each at the front and the back doors of the house. All of them were armed with pistols and submachine guns.

In addition, there was a small concrete block-house about twenty yards from the back right-

hand corner of the outside fence. Two more guards were posted on the low roof of this structure, hidden from view by trees.

Garrison asked Balzer about it.

"The laboratory has its own electrical generator plant in case the main lines are downed by bombing, sabotage, or storms," he informed them.

"What about inside the house?" Casino asked.

"Swarming with Gestapo," Balzer said.

Garrison held his briefing in a hollow. "We're going to watch this place night and day for a few days. Three shifts, around the clock. Casey, you and the Chief take the first hitch. Goniff and Casino will relieve you. The Actor and I will take the last shift. Keep your eyes open. I don't have to tell you what to do. I'll want a detailed report on everything that happens down there. Even if a man spits."

The Gorillas nodded confidently. They did not need instructions. This work was as natural to them as eating and breathing.

At Balzer's cottage they had exchanged their German carbines for pistols, and the Czech had given them a pair of high-powered field glasses which Garrison now handed over to his guard detail.

They returned to Balzer's place and the Americans waited in the underground communications center while Balzer went to get Kati so that Garrison could talk to her.

The girl surprised him. She was older than he had expected—perhaps twenty-eight or twenty-nine—and very pretty, although her hair was worn in simple braids over the top of her head and she wore no makeup. Her blouse and peasant skirt were shapeless and not at all becoming.

The thing that surprised him the most was her eyes. They were very blue and bright. Garrison could hardly believe what Balzer had said, that she had the mind of a child. She looked very intelligent. But after he talked to her for a while, it seemed that Balzer was right.

She curtsied to him like a little girl, and she smiled and giggled frequently. It took patient questioning to get the information that he wanted from her.

Kati visited the laboratory three times a week with her dogcart to deliver fresh laundry and to pick up dirty linen. Every Wednesday she spent a full afternoon inside the house in a small upstairs room across from Professor Kropotkin's workroom, sewing for the Germans as well as the professor. She often spoke to him. Sometimes when he was tired after working for many hours in the laboratory, he would come into her sewing room and sit down and smoke his pipe. Kati said he was a kind, friendly man. She liked him very much.

"The Germans permit this?" Garrison asked. "They let you talk to the professor alone?"

Kati giggled. "The Germans don't worry about me. They call me a. . . ." She said a word in Czechoslovakian that Garrison did not understand. He looked at Balzer.

The Czech translated it for him. "They call her 'the moron.'"

Kati giggled again and brushed back her blond hair with one hand.

"You like the professor very much, Kati?" Garrison said. "Do you like him better than you like the Germans?"

The smile left her face for the first time. "Oh, yes. The soldiers treat me all right, but they are not good men. They came here and killed many of our people. I like Professor Kropotkin."

Balzer took it from there. Patiently and seriously he explained to the girl that Garrison and his American friends were there to help rescue Professor Kropotkin from the Germans.

"If he does not get away from them soon, they will kill him. Do you understand?"

She nodded.

"If you help us save Professor Kropotkin, then the war will be over soon, and the Germans will leave Czechoslovakia for good." Balzer smiled. "You'd like that, wouldn't you?"

Her face beamed happily and she clapped her hands together. "Yes, I would like that very much."

Garrison looked at Balzer. "Do you have equipment here for microfilming documents?"

"We have everything you need," Balzer replied with pride. "It was smuggled in bolt by bolt from England."

"Good!" Garrison said. "I want to type out a message for Jules Kropotkin. You'll transfer it to microfilm, and Kati will smuggle it into the lab."

Casino frowned. "But how's he gonna read it?"

"Simple," Balzer said. He went to a cabinet and came back with a large, showy woman's brooch with rhinestones on it. The brooch broke into two parts, revealing a secret compartment inside it.

"The film goes in here," he explained. He put the two parts together again and pointed to a stone larger than the others in the middle of the pin. "This is a fine precision lens, very high-powered." He handed it to Casino. "Look."

Casino put his eye to the little stone and got the surprise of his life. Holding it up against the glare of a light bulb, he was able to read quite clearly a copy of the American Declaration of Independence in its entirety.

Balzer grinned and held up a sliver of microfilm no larger than the nail of his little finger. "All on this."

Garrison nodded. "Let's get to work."

While Garrison was composing his message to Jules Kropotkin, the other Americans ate a meal of bread and wine supplied by their Czech host.

The Actor's appetite was not good, and Balzer asked him, "Is there something wrong with the food?"

"No." The Actor shook his handsome head. "I'm worried, Balzer. That girl . . . are you positive she can be trusted?"

"I would stake my life on it. Why?"

"I can't explain it," the Actor said slowly. "In America we call it a 'hunch.' "

"Knock it off, Actor," Casino said, mumbling through a mouthful of food.

"No. I'm serious. There's something not quite right about Kati. I know it. Listen, when you've been a con man as long as I have, you get so you can recognize a phony when you meet one."

The other Gorillas stopped laughing. They knew exactly what the Actor meant.

"You really figure the kid is a phony?" Goniff asked anxiously.

"I have a bad feeling about her," the Actor said. "She's not playing square with us."

Now the rest of them had no appetite.

8.

CASEY GETS A JOB

KATI TOOK the microfilm message to Jules Kropotkin the following Wednesday. After delivering the Germans' laundry, she went to the small room off the laboratory and did her weekly sewing. It was several hours before she had an opportunity to see the professor alone.

She was almost finished with her chores when he strolled in, smoking his pipe, and leaned against the doorjamb. A Gestapo man was hovering in the hall behind him.

111

"And how are you today, Kati, my dear?" he asked.

"The same as ever, sir," she answered without looking up. After a time she put down the shirt she was working on and smiled. "See what I have, Professor." She pointed to her brooch.

"That's lovely, Kati," he said. "Where did you get it?"

"I found it in the road."

A dark, thin-faced Gestapo man shouldered his way past Kropotkin into the room. "Let me see that," he snapped.

Kati whimpered like a child and held both hands over the brooch where it was pinned to her blouse.

"No, you can't have it. It's mine!" she cried. "I didn't steal it."

The man held out his hand. "Give it here, Kati!"

"Let the girl alone, Schroeder," Kropotkin protested. "It's only costume jewelry."

Schroeder slapped her hands down and removed the brooch. He held it up to the light of the window for examination. Then he smirked and dropped it into her lap.

"Junk."

He yawned and walked out of the room, his footsteps fading down the long hallway. Kati was still whimpering.

"It's not junk! It's beautiful!" she wailed.

"Of course it's beautiful, my dear." Kropotkin came over and put a comforting arm about her shoulders.

She held the brooch up close to his face. "See the wonderful diamonds. Look at the big one in the middle."

Kropotkin pulled back as she almost shoved the brooch into his eye.

She kept nodding her head and urging him. "Look. Look into it. See the pretty diamond."

Abruptly it dawned on him what she was doing. Quickly he took the brooch and put it to his eye.

When he lowered it again his face was red and his eyes bright with excitement. He went to the door and peered up and down the hall. Then he took out a notebook and tore out a sheet of paper.

Leaning against the wall, he wrote hurriedly on the paper with a short pencil. When he was done he folded the paper twice and gave it to the girl.

"Put it in your shoe, Kati. They never search you, do they?"

She shook her head. "Not anymore."

Two hours later the professor's note was in Garrison's hands. It read:

> When the Nazis captured me I had no idea where Emile was. But a year ago I came into some new information. I can help you find Emile, but you must get me out of here before I can do so. *This must be done my way!*

Garrison frowned. "I don't like it. Emile is the one we should locate first."

"Sure," the Actor agreed. "Once we spring

Jules we'll have the whole German Army and the Gestapo breathing down our necks. It's crazy."

Garrison shrugged. "We don't have any choice, though. He's pretty definite about it. 'This must be done my way!' "

He spread out a sheaf of reports that his men had prepared based on their careful observations of the chalet where Professor Kropotkin was a prisoner. He circled one item that appeared in each of the reports over a period of three days.

"This looks like our best bet," he said. "At exactly ten o'clock every night a command car with an S.S. colonel pulls up to the main gate. The colonel goes inside and talks with Kropotkin and his Gestapo shadows." He looked at Goniff. "How do you know that?"

"One night they left the laboratory blinds up. We could see inside with the field glasses."

Garrison nodded. "As I see it, the one weak link in their defenses is the generator that supplies their electrical power."

"Check," Casino said. "If we knock out the generator, we cut off their juice. No lights. No power for that electric fence."

"What we have to do is create a diversion to keep those roving patrols outside the fence busy," Garrison said. "Then we go in the back way and take out the professor."

Casey didn't like it. "Yeah. Okay, warden, but what about the guards inside the house—them Gestapo goons that are always with Kropotkin?"

Garrison walked over to Casey and put a hand on his shoulder. "That's where you fit in. You're going to be our 'insurance man' on the inside."

"Come again?" The little man blinked.

"According to your record, you're supposed to be the greatest impersonator in the business."

Casey puffed out his chest. "You tell 'em, Lieutenant."

Garrison pointed to Kati, who was standing quietly to one side. "Do you think you could double for Kati?"

116

Casey did not answer right away. In his most professional manner he walked around the girl several times, studying her from various angles and scratching his chin.

"Take off your shoes, Kati," he instructed her. "Fine. Now stand back to back with me."

Garrison measured them with his eyes. "You're about an inch taller than Kati."

"That don't matter," Casey said. "They'll never notice."

"You think you can do it?"

Casey snapped his fingers. "A cinch."

Casino and Goniff hooted. "You got to be kidding," Casino said. "You actually think you can pass yourself off as this cute doll?"

"I can do it," Casey said with confidence. "Of course, I'll need the right equipment." He looked to Balzer. "Can the underground dig me up a kit of theatrical makeup and a blond wig?"

"I think that can be arranged," the Czech said.

"Fine. And I'll want some photographs of Kati.

117

From a lot of different angles."

"We'll take care of that," Garrison said. He turned to Kati. "You said there are two Gestapo agents with Kropotkin at all times?"

"Most of the time," she said. "Oh, they leave him alone sometimes, like when he comes in to visit me while I'm sewing. But they're never very far away."

Garrison frowned. "Are there any other guards inside the house?"

She thought it over for a minute. "There is a couple—a man and wife, I think—who do the cooking and take care of the house. I have seen the man serve the professor and the Gestapo men lunch. The professor is not allowed to go down-stairs."

Garrison shook his head. "Well, I guess that's all we have to know for now. All we can do now is mark time until next Wednesday." He patted Kati's arm. "You've been a big help to us, Kati. Thank you."

She giggled like a pleased child and clapped her hands. "Oh, this is such fun! I can't wait until Wednesday so we can play more games!"

Casino and Goniff looked at her with sickly grins. When she had left, Casino shook his head and groaned.

" 'Games,' she says!" He tapped the side of his head with a finger. "That kid is missing a lot of nuts and bolts upstairs."

"Yeah," Goniff agreed. He looked at the Actor. "You still think she ain't on the level?"

The Actor was puzzled. "I don't know. I just don't know. . . . There's something wrong about her. I'd lay money on that. But I can't figure out what it is."

"That's crazy," Casey argued. "If she was working with the Germans, she could have put the finger on us long before this. Right, warden?"

Garrison was disturbed. "It would seem so." He glanced at Balzer. "Just how much do you know about Kati?"

119

The Czech underground leader shrugged. "Not much. Only that she's been living with the old woman for a little over a year now. I told you she has done several small favors for the underground. If she were a traitor she'd have turned us all in by now."

"That's an old sucker's game," the Actor said dryly. "You let the mark win a couple of small pots. Then when he starts to put up real big money, you deal yourself a royal flush."

"How true," Goniff admitted gloomily.

A chill ran up Garrison's spine. It was true. The stakes in this game were very high. If they lost, the Nazis would win Emile Kropotkin—and Garrison's Gorillas!

9.

THE STRANGE
SET OF TWINS

The following Wednesday morning Casey shut himself up with Kati for three hours in the secret room underneath Balzer's cottage. Finally the two of them presented themselves for inspection.

A chorus of astonished exclamations greeted them. Garrison could not believe his eyes! Casey had worked a miracle with a little greasepaint, powder, and rouge. Unless you studied the two people very closely and knew what you were looking for, it was almost impossible to tell which was

121

Kati and which was Casey.

One of the Katis walked over to Goniff and pinched his cheek. "You're cute, you little ape." The voice and the giggle were perfect.

"Casey?" Goniff asked, not at all certain who it was.

The other Gorillas and the real Kati laughed uproariously. Goniff blushed.

"You could have fooled me," he mumbled.

Garrison shook his head wonderingly. "It's amazing, Casey. I don't know how you do it."

"That's why they called me the 'Great Impersonator,'" Casey said in his natural voice.

Balzer stared at Casey curiously. "Tell me, Mr. Casey—with your great talent, you could have made a fortune in my country as a performer on the stage and in the circus. Why—"

"He could have been a star in the United States, too," Garrison interrupted, his voice sarcastic. "Instead he threw it away for a jail cell and a life sentence."

All of the Gorillas hung their heads and were silent. Garrison could guess what they were thinking. Each of them possessed a talent which, put to work honestly instead of dishonestly, would easily have made them successful and highly respected citizens.

As was her custom every Wednesday morning, the real Kati took her dogcart loaded with clean laundry and uniforms up to the heavily guarded gate of the chalet. All of the guards greeted her in friendly fashion and helped her unload the fresh linen and load the cart with bags of dirty laundry. Kati gave the big shaggy dog a pat on the hindquarters and sent him trotting back down the road to the shack where she lived with the old woman. Then she was passed through the two gates, so that she could perform her weekly sewing chores inside the house.

The door of the little room where she worked was usually kept open, but the girl was in a singing mood that day. After listening to her high

124

soprano voice for half an hour, one of the Gestapo men who was watching Professor Kropotkin at work on an experiment got up and closed the door irritably.

"A nice girl," he grumbled, "but that voice!"

At four o'clock in the afternoon the guards on the gates and on roving patrol, as well as the two soldiers at the generator house, were relieved.

A half hour later Craig Garrison lay on the hill overlooking the house, watching through his field glasses. Shortly after, Casey, disguised as Kati, the laundry girl, approached the gate, walking alone.

"Hello, there, Kati!" one of the newly arrived soldiers said. "You're late today."

"I delivered the laundry this morning," Casey said in Kati's voice. "But I had to go home and help the old woman. Now I'm back to sew on your buttons and patch your socks."

The soldiers laughed. "Good old Kati," one of them said as he opened the gate. "I don't know how we would get along without you."

Another German went inside the guard shack and got a sack of clothing that needed mending. Casey took the sack and passed through the gates, strolling unhurriedly toward the house. His heart was hammering in his chest.

All that had to happen now, he thought, was for one of the Gestapo men to be looking out an upstairs window! The party would be over even before it had started!

The guard at the front door grinned and opened the door. "And how are you today, Kati?"

Casey smiled sweetly. "I'm fine, thank you."

Inside the house he went down a dark hallway until he found the stairs. In the upper hall he took out his pistol and snapped off the safety. The open door of the laboratory was only a few steps away. He looked at the closed door of the little room across the hall where the real Kati was sewing.

The two Gestapo men were watching Pro-

126

fessor Kropotkin nervously as he held a foaming test tube over the flame of a Bunsen burner.

"Can that thing explode?" one of them asked.

"It's possible," Kropotkin admitted.

The tall, blond one heard a noise behind him and looked over his shoulder. It was Kati.

"Are you through for the day?" he asked her.

"Not quite." Casey spoke in his natural voice. He brought out the gun from behind the sack of clothing he was holding.

Both Gestapo men whirled about, staring at a wild phenomenon. The face and form of Kati the laundry girl, but the voice of a man!

"Don't go for your gun!" Casey said sharply in German as one man's hand moved toward his holster. "You're dead if you do." He walked toward them. "Now turn around."

The Germans obeyed. Casey chopped the blond one at the base of the neck with the barrel of his pistol. Then the other. They slumped to the floor without a sound.

Professor Kropotkin was bewildered. "I—I don't understand," he said. "Who are you?"

At that instant the real Kati crossed the hall and came into the laboratory. Kropotkin stared at the two identical figures in astonishment.

"It's black magic," he whispered.

"No, Professor, just good makeup." Casey grinned and peeled off his wig.

A thought came to the professor then. "You must be one of the American agents."

"Right, Professor," Casey said. "We're going to get you out of here tonight." He spoke to the girl. "Kati, you go out and stand guard at the stairs in case we get unexpected company."

When she had left the room he started to strip off his disguise. "You must have some strong rope around here. We'll have to bind and gag these two."

The professor nodded. "In the cupboard." He hurried to get it.

The smaller of the unconscious Germans was

about Casey's size. They undressed him before they tied him up and Casey put on his clothing. When the two Gestapo men were trussed securely, Casey dragged them into a closet at the back of the room and shut the door.

"They'll keep nicely in there until we lam out of this joint," he said.

Professor Kropotkin spoke excellent English, but this he did not understand at all.

"*Lam?* Out of this *joint?* I beg your pardon."

Casey laughed. "Just some expressions the boys used at the college I went to, Professor."

Kropotkin smiled. "Ah, yes. American slang."

Casey went to the door and signaled for Kati to come in from the hall. He took her hands and patted them.

"You're a good, brave girl," he told her. "You did everything just fine. Now, you go back to your work, just as if nothing happened. At your regular time, you pack up and leave."

The professor was anxious. "How are we going

to get out of here through that army of soldiers?"
he asked.

"Keep cool, Professor. We have a long wait.
The action won't start until after dark. . . . Listen,
are any of these Nazi goons likely to come up to
the lab for any reason?"

Kropotkin shook his head. "No. But once every
hour on the hour Werner reports to the officer of
the guard on the phone."

"Werner?"

Kropotkin pointed to the closet. "The blond
one."

Casey looked at his watch. "I can handle that.
What's he say?"

"Oh, not much. Something such as, 'Werner
here. Everything is fine.' He has a high-pitched
voice."

Kropotkin thought of something else. "There's
one more problem. At six thirty the couple who
take care of this house will be serving dinner
up here."

130

Casey frowned. "That's not so good, is it?" He gave the matter some thought. "Hmmm . . . I wonder. . . ." He picked up the blond wig he had used in his impersonation. "Professor, get me a pair of scissors. I'm gonna give a haircut."

The custodians of the house were Fritz Keppler and his wife Bertha. They were trusted employees of the Gestapo. With their beady eyes and hunched shoulders, they looked like a pair of vultures.

At the customary hour of six thirty in the evening they loaded the covered food bowls onto two trays and carried them upstairs to the laboratory.

Casey and the professor were standing at the rear of the room with their backs to the door, feeding some guinea pigs that lived in tiered cages against the back wall. Casey was wearing Werner's clothing and the blond wig he had cut down. Fritz and Bertha scarcely gave him a second look.

They arranged the bowls and dishes on a table

and set three places. As she laid down the knives and forks, Bertha inquired, "Where is Max?"

Professor Kropotkin nodded toward the bathroom at one side of the laboratory. Behind the closed door was the muffled roar of a shower.

"He's bathing," he said. "I never knew a man who took so many baths."

The woman grunted and finished setting the table. When they were gone Kropotkin sagged against the wall.

"That was very close, Mr. Casey," he said.

"You think that was close, Prof, wait until the main event begins," Casey said grimly.

10.

BREAK-OUT!

THE LITTLE concrete blockhouse that contained the generator system was set back near the fringe of the woods. It was a squat, ugly structure, and in the daytime in the summer months the sun beating down on its flat, white roof made the interior as hot as an oven. Twice the generators had burned out because of overheating. To cure that, the Germans had planted shade trees around the blockhouse. The trees screened out the sunlight—and they also screened off the blockhouse from the soldiers guarding the main house and the fence.

Craig Garrison was very grateful for this fact as he and the Chief crawled through the high grass at the edge of the forest. The Germans guarding the blockhouse were two dark, helmeted silhouettes. They were sitting on the roof of the building with their feet dangling over the side, facing the house.

The deep, throbbing hum of the generators muffled any small sounds that the Americans made as they slithered up to the back of the structure. Garrison and the Chief stood up behind the generator house. The flat roof was about chest high. As silently as shadows they pulled themselves up onto the flat concrete slab. It was ten feet across to the Germans, who were smoking cigarettes and talking in quiet voices about the latest war news.

Garrison nodded and they sprang like cats. The big Indian's leather garrote whizzed through the

night air. It closed on one soldier's throat, choking off his outcry.

Garrison clamped a headlock on his man, his powerful forearm clenched tight against the Nazi's windpipe. He held the grip until the soldier's body went limp.

They dragged the Germans inside the blockhouse. Then Garrison cupped his hands to his mouth and made a cry like a hoot owl. Minutes later Casino came out of the shadow of the woods.

"Okay, it's all yours," Garrison told him. "You're the electrical expert. Sure you know what to do?"

Casino nodded. "I blow the whole works at ten sharp."

At precisely 9:45 P.M. S.S. Col. Johann Eberhart's command car was rolling over the desolate road that led to the chalet where Jules Kropotkin was imprisoned. For nineteen months Eberhart had been assigned to the Kropotkin case. His mission: Find Emile Kropotkin, unite the two brother scientists, and wring the secret of formula Fear 1-X out of them. He was no closer to his goal this night than he had been when he started. This nightly inspection tour was a bore, too. The colonel yawned. Anyway, it was better than duty on the Eastern front!

Unexpectedly Eberhart was thrown forward in the backseat as his driver came down on the brakes very hard.

"Dummkopf!" he roared. "What are you trying to do, kill me?"

"I'm sorry, sir," the corporal apologized. "But look!"

Colonel Eberhart peered out through the windshield. Lying in the middle of the road in the glare of the command car's headlights was a man wearing a German Army uniform. He was sprawled alongside a bicycle.

"Hit-and-run!" the colonel said grimly. "Come, Stolz, we'd better have a look at him."

The two men got out of the car and walked

up to the still form in the road.

"Roll him over," Eberhart ordered his driver. "Let's have a look at his face."

Stolz bent down and grabbed one of the man's shoulders. As he turned him over, the "victim" suddenly came to life. It was the Actor. He swung his right arm in a wide arc and clipped the driver under the chin with the edge of his hand. Stolz gagged and clutched at his throat. He collapsed in the road, choking.

Cursing, the colonel sprang back and drew his Luger pistol. The Actor just sat there in the road.

"You filthy swine!" Eberhart said angrily. "What is the meaning of this? Speak up or I'll kill you!"

His finger tightened on the trigger. He did not hear the Chief come up behind him until it was too late. A karate chop sent the Luger spinning into the bushes at the side of the road. The long, wicked knife flashed in the glare of the headlights. And Colonel Johann Eberhart blacked out.

Quickly the Gorillas stripped off the Germans' uniforms and put them on. The Actor put on the colonel's peaked cap at a jaunty angle, buckled the heavy leather belt, and admired his gleaming black boots.

"Really quite a good fit, don't you think?" he asked the Chief.

The big Indian grunted and looked down unhappily at himself. The uniform of the German driver was much too small for him.

"I see what you mean," the Actor said. "But it won't be noticed as long as you stay in the car."

They dumped the Germans into the bushes and got into the command car with the Chief at the wheel.

It was one minute before ten o'clock when they drove up to the gate at the chalet. The guards came to attention and saluted. The Actor returned the salute, careful to keep his face in the shadow.

139

The outer gate swung open and the Chief eased the long car half through it. Then the inner gate swung open. He inched the car forward again. At ten o'clock all the lights in the house and on the fences dimmed, flickered, and went out.

"Stop!" the Actor roared.

The command car was so situated that the front end prevented the inner gate from being shut, while the rear bumper blocked the outer gate. The German guards were talking excitedly and shining their flashlights all around. A sergeant hurried up to the command car and said in an apologetic voice, "Colonel, will you please move on so that we can shut the gates?"

The Actor threw open the door, almost knocking the German down, and got out of the car. "Why have the lights gone out?" he shouted. "Who is responsible for this breach of security?"

The Actor's impression of a furious Prussian officer was perfect, and the sergeant backed off.

"I don't know, sir," he stammered. "Nothing like this has ever happened before."

The Actor stamped his feet in anger. "Well, it's happening now, and I'm going to get to the bottom of it at once. Where is the officer of the guard?" He headed toward the sentry box outside the gate with the sergeant trailing after him.

"Please, Colonel, the car," he pleaded. "It must be moved."

The Actor ignored him. "Officer of the guard! Where is he?"

"He's making an inspection tour of the roving patrols around the fence."

"Get him here at once!" the Actor shouted. "I want every man on duty here assembled at once. We're going to find out who is responsible for this inexcusable inefficiency."

"Yes, sir." The sergeant took a whistle out of his pocket and blew it shrilly to call in the sentries patrolling outside the fence.

When the coast was clear behind the house,

Casino went into his act. Scaling the two high fences was easy for the man who had been a notorious cat burglar in civilian life. Inside the grounds, he ran to the house and scrambled up the thick ivy that grew up the rough brick wall. He reached an open second-story window and climbed through. The glare of a flashlight blinded him.

"Casino!" Casey's voice said. "The Marines have landed, Professor."

"What has happened?" Kropotkin asked nervously. "The lights?"

"Courtesy of Garrison's Gorillas," Casino said lightly. "Come on. We don't have no time for talk now. How do we get downstairs?"

"Follow me," Casey said. He led them out into the hall and to the top of the stairs. He shone the flashlight down the stairs and spotlighted two German soldiers armed with submachine guns. They were the guards who had been posted at the front and back doors.

"Watch it!" he yelled and flattened himself against the wall as one of the Germans fired a burst from his submachine gun. Casino threw himself against Professor Kropotkin and knocked him to the floor. A hail of bullets shattered the plaster of the wall behind them.

Casey returned the fire, and the Germans ducked away from the stairs. Casey got down on his knees and crawled over to Casino and Kropotkin.

"Everybody over here still in one piece?" he whispered.

Casino nodded. "We're okay. What happens now?"

They ducked their heads as another volley from the Nazi submachine guns riddled the air over their prone forms. Casino and Casey fired their pistols at the winking muzzle blasts in the darkness below.

"You and the professor better go back down the way you came in," Casey told Casino. "I'll keep these guys busy in here until you're in the clear."

Casino frowned. "What about you? You get left holding a tiger by the tail, and you can't let go of it."

"You know the rules, Casino," Casey said grimly. "The professor is the only one of us who counts right now. Get going."

Casey fired a couple more rounds down the dark stairwell as Casino and Kropotkin crawled back to the laboratory.

"Prof, how are you at climbing up and down walls?" Casino asked. "Ever done any second-story work?"

"I beg your pardon?" Kropotkin said.

Casino laughed. "Never mind. Throw one leg over the windowsill and grab hold of the ivy. It's as strong as rope."

"I'll do my best," Kropotkin said, gritting his teeth. He took a deep breath and climbed out.

"Say, that was pretty good, Prof," Casino said

as they dropped to the earth. "Maybe someday you and I can go into partnership."

"My word!" the professor gasped. "You Americans are so hard to understand."

"Freedom, Professor," Casino said. "You understand that."

"It has been so long since I heard that word," Kropotkin said sadly. *"Freedom*—it sounds so wonderful."

"Now, for your second lesson." Casino led the way back to the inner fence. With a boost from Casino, the professor managed to scramble over the top. He landed hard on the other side.

Casino bent down beside him anxiously. "You all right, Prof?"

Kropotkin gulped in air. "Yes . . . just had the wind knocked out of me."

"No time for rest," Casino told him. He looked up anxiously at the high-tension wires running along the top of the outer fence. "If the Germans get the power on before we make it back over, that's all there is, brother!"

He gave the shaky professor another boost and Kropotkin hauled himself over the outer fence like a sack of potatoes. This time he landed on his hands and knees.

"Good boy!" Casino patted his back. "We made it." He pulled Kropotkin to his feet and they ran for the woods.

Garrison and Goniff were waiting for them. The lieutenant was not happy. "We heard the shooting in the house and figured you got fouled up," he said. "What happened?"

"The two goons who were guarding the doors jumped us as we were starting down the stairs," Casino told him. "Casey stayed behind to fight rear guard."

Garrison stared toward the house. The shooting had stopped. "Looks like poor Casey has had it," he said sadly.

"What about the Actor and the Chief?" Casino asked him.

146

"They can take care of themselves," Garrison said. "Right now the important thing is to get Professor Kropotkin stashed away where the Germans can't find him."

The Actor was enjoying the role he was playing. He had all the Germans lined up at attention, including the first lieutenant in charge of the detachment. He marched up and down in front of them, raving and ranting and shaking his fist.

"Gross incompetency, Lieutenant!" he said for the tenth time.

Then the sound of shooting came from the direction of the house. The Actor decided it was time to make a break.

"There's trouble at the laboratory!" he screamed. "All right, you men, to the house! On the double."

The formation broke up and poured through the gate. The Actor ran along with the soldiers for a while, letting himself fall behind. In the darkness and excitement, no one noticed. Then he ran back to the command car and got in beside the Chief.

"Let's get out of here *fast!*"

11.

THE REAL EMILE

THEY ALL MET back in the secret room beneath the floor of Balzer's hut. Tears came to the eyes of the underground leader as he embraced the professor.

"All these months we have thought of nothing else but of the glorious day when you would be freed from the Nazis' clutches," he said. He looked gratefully at Garrison and the other Americans. "We owe our thanks to you, Lieutenant, and to your brave men."

"It's not over yet, Balzer," Garrison reminded him. "There is still much danger."

"Yes, of course," Balzer said. "It is all arranged. Just ten miles away, a small plane is waiting in a secret underground airstrip in the deep woods. We must take Professor Kropotkin there at once. In a few hours he will be safe in Switzerland."

"No," Kropotkin said curtly. "I won't leave without Emile."

"I'm sorry, Professor," Garrison said in a firm voice, "but you must follow my orders. Don't worry about your brother. We'll find him and get him out safely, too. Now, suppose you tell us where we can find Emile."

Jules Kropotkin was behaving very strangely. He could not look Garrison in the eye. "In due time," he said in a low voice.

"There is no time!" Garrison said. "Within a few hours the German Army will throw a cordon around this whole area. Where is your brother hiding? Is it around here?"

Kropotkin avoided the question and changed the subject. "Where is Kati? She must go with me. When they find those Gestapo men tied up in the closet, they will identify her as an accomplice of the Americans."

"She'll be here any minute," Balzer told him. "I sent two of our people to bring her back here."

Garrison was becoming irritable with the professor. "Professor Kropotkin, will you answer my question, please? Where is your brother Emile hiding?"

Kropotkin hung his head. "I can't tell you now," he said in a low voice.

"You can't tell us!" Casino grabbed him by the lapels of his coat and dragged him out of the chair. "Are you some kind of nut? We risked our necks to save your hide. We lost one of our guys doing it! Now you play cute with us. I ought to—" He raised a hand threateningly.

Garrison stepped between them. "At ease, Casino. No rough stuff."

"But, warden!"

"He's right, Lieutenant," Goniff said. The other Gorillas gathered around them.

"Professor Kropotkin," Garrison said gently. "What's wrong? Why won't you tell us where to find your brother?"

At that instant the two underground members who had been sent to get Kati returned. They were alone.

"She wouldn't come with us," one of them said. "The old lady took a bad spell, and they called the doctor. Kati says she'll be along in a little while."

Garrison frowned at Balzer. "The little idiot! Doesn't she realize the danger she's in every minute that she stays there?"

Balzer was already on his way up the stairs. "I'll bring her back, even if I have to carry her."

"Such a good, kind girl, my Kati," Kropotkin said softly to himself. "Such a brave girl."

Garrison looked at the professor strangely. A

wild idea was forming in his mind, an idea so beyond belief that he dared not say it to the others. They waited in silence until Balzer returned. His face was pale.

"She is gone," he said in a hoarse voice. "The Germans came and took her. I almost got caught by a patrol on my way back here." He put a hand on Garrison's arm. "I also have some news for you, Lieutenant. Your man, Casey—he is alive, at least. The Germans have him up at the lab." His eyes fell. "They are interrogating him."

Garrison winced. They all knew what that meant! Gestapo interrogation!

"He would have been better off dead," Goniff said.

Kropotkin was crying. "Kati! They have her there as well?"

"I'm afraid so," Balzer said, looking away.

"War is a very rough game," Garrison said bitterly. "People get killed." He took a deep breath and put Kati and Casey out of his mind.

153

"No more stalling around, Kropotkin. Get ready to leave here with Balzer and his men and catch that plane."

The professor covered his face with his hands. "You don't understand, Lieutenant Garrison. Emile Kropotkin. . . . Kati *is* Emile!"

Garrison was speechless. His hunch was not so wild after all.

The other Gorillas and Balzer and his men gaped at Jules Kropotkin as if he were a madman.

"What did you say?" Balzer asked in a shocked voice.

The professor looked up at them. "I have no brother. I never did. My sister *Emily* and I are the scientific team that wrote all those papers that made us known to the world."

"J. and E. Kropotkin . . . that is how you always signed them," Balzer said.

"Yes. Emily felt that our theories would be accepted more readily if the world's scientists thought she was a man. It was not hard to deceive

154

people. We lived a quiet life in the country. No one came to interview us or to take our photographs. Only our close friends knew anything about us.

"Then, when just before the war our experiments with Fear One-X serum came to the attention of the Czechoslovakian government, the authorities put a tight web of security around us.

"If there had only been a little more time our government could have produced the serum and used it against the invading Germans. But it was too late. The Nazi armies were at the gates of Prague. Our laboratory was destroyed. Our papers were burned. Emily memorized one half of the formula. I memorized the other. All of our official records were changed to throw the Germans off the scent. They knew about Fear One-X through their spies, but they didn't know that E. Kropotkin was a woman. A false birth certificate was placed in the public records for 'Emile Kropotkin.' Then Emily was placed in an institution for the mentally retarded under the name of Kati Kursik. Last year an old friend in government who was in on the secret arranged for Kati to be placed in the home of the old woman near here as a companion and nurse. The rest of the tale you already know."

"Amazing!" Balzer gasped. "And all this time we thought the poor girl had the brain of a child. Imagine, one of the most brilliant minds in the world!"

Goniff grinned. "We told you, warden. She was hiding right under the noses of the Germans, where they never thought to look for her."

"I told you she was a phony," the Actor said with satisfaction.

"And now they have her, and they don't even know it," Garrison said grimly.

"It is very bad," Balzer said. "Suppose they torture her? Suppose they find out who she really is? They will make her give them the other part of the formula."

"And Fear One-X will contaminate every major water supply the Allies have. The Germans will conquer the world without firing another shot," Kropotkin said.

Garrison smashed a fist down hard on the table. "We've got to get her away from them."

The Actor shook his head. "You can pull that kind of caper once and get away with it, but it would never work again. They'd be ready for us the next time."

Garrison knew he was right. "There has to be some way," he insisted.

Balzer had a suggestion. "I can round up a force of underground fighters."

"No good," one of his men said. "Heavy reinforcements have already arrived at the house. There are heavy machine guns set up on the roof and two tanks inside the fence."

"They expect us to attack again," Garrison said. "They're using Casey and Kati as bait."

He slumped down in a chair. "What's the use

of kidding ourselves? We're beat. There's only one thing to do now."

He hated to even think about it. The last of his secret orders covered just such a situation as this. Neither Kropotkin was to be allowed to remain in German possession. It was too risky. He turned to Balzer.

"Warm up the transmitter. I have to send a message to headquarters in London. Two words: 'Kill—destroy.' "

"What does that mean?" Kropotkin asked tersely.

"It means that the Allied air forces will send bombers over to destroy the laboratory."

"And my poor Emily!" the professor cried. "No, Lieutenant! There has to be another way."

"If anyone has any answers that I don't have, speak up now."

Balzer was sitting at the shortwave radio transmitter, twirling the dials. Professor Kropotkin was pacing up and down, his hands deep in the pockets of his jacket. One hand came out of a pocket, holding a bottle containing liquid. He jiggled it up and down nervously as he walked.

Garrison watched him curiously. "What's in that bottle, Professor?" he asked.

Kropotkin stopped and blinked at the bottle in his hand. "What? This? It is what remains of the small quantity of Fear One-X that Emily and I distilled before we fled from the Germans. When I escaped from the chalet, I thought it best to take it with me."

Garrison's eyes gleamed with excitement. He walked over and took the bottle from Kropotkin, holding it up to the light. It was thick and milky.

"How much of the serum is there in this bottle?" he asked.

"Enough to turn a city of twenty thousand people mad with fear," the professor answered.

Garrison turned to Balzer. "Where does the water that supplies the chalet come from?"

Balzer shrugged. "From the natural springs

160

on the tall mountain behind the house. The original owners of the house piped it in. When the Germans came here they put a small dam up there to form a reservoir so that they could supply their army encampment in the valley."

Garrison twirled the bottle in his fingers. "How many soldiers do they have in the camp?"

"Close to a full division. It is the headquarters for all of the German occupation troops in this part of Europe."

Balzer called into the mike in front of him. "Dragonfly calling Green Dragon. . . . Come in, Green Dragon. . . ."

Garrison stopped him. "Forget that call to London. I don't think we're going to need any help from the Air Force after all. . . . Balzer, take us to that reservoir at once."

He planted a kiss on the bottle of Fear 1-X.

12.

ATTACK
IN DARKNESS

THE RESERVOIR and the dam were enclosed behind a high wire fence topped with barbed wire. At either end of the dam was a sentry tower manned by a soldier behind a .50 caliber machine gun. When the Nazis had first set up their camp in the valley, the little dam had been blown up twice by saboteurs. Now it was fenced in and guarded. Spotlights on all four sides of the towers bathed the open ground around them, so that it was impossible for any enemy to sneak up on them.

Balzer, Garrison, and the Gorillas surveyed the situation from a thick clump of woods about fifty yards from one of the towers.

"We can pick off the guards easily with a rifle fitted with a telescopic sight," Balzer suggested.

"No good," Garrison said. "The shots would be heard by the patrols that cover the area. . . . Casino, see if you can locate the wires that feed power to those lights."

Ten minutes later Casino came back. "I found 'em, warden. You want I should cut them?"

Garrison thought about it a moment and decided it would be too risky. "They may have a signal system set up in case any saboteurs get the same idea. Probably a field telephone. If the lights go out they phone for help. . . . No, what I want to do is just knock out the lights on one tower for a few minutes. Can you work it out, Casino?"

Casino's forehead was wrinkled in deep thought. "Yeah, I can do it." From his back pocket he took a canvas roll that contained a set of electrician's tools, all of them scaled down to miniature size for easy carrying.

"Goniff, you go with him and lend a hand," Garrison ordered. He put an arm around the Chief's shoulders. "Here's what I want you to do. . . ."

Five minutes later the spotlights on the tower nearest to where they were concealed blacked out. The lights on the other tower still burned brightly.

The sentry in the lighted tower called across the dam. "Erich, what happened?"

"Just a temporary failure, I think," the other German called back. "Your lights are still on. It's happened before. We'll give it a few minutes before we report a power failure."

He turned and flashed his hand torch down on the ground around the tower. By mere inches, the beam just missed the dark figure flattened out against the base of the tower. The German turned off the torch and resumed his conversation with the guard at the other end of the dam.

The dark figure started to climb silently up the crisscrossed beams that supported the sentry box on stiltlike legs. He reached the top. Slowly his eyes rose over the side of the open box. The guard had his back to that side.

The German heard a soft whirring noise that sounded like a night insect. Like a whip the leather garrote snapped around his throat and cut off air and sound. The Chief lowered the limp body to the floor of the shack and stripped off the man's uniform jacket and helmet.

Across the dam, the other German yelled, "Hey! You over there! You're awfully quiet! Erich, are you all right?" His hand reached for the field telephone on the wall of the sentry box.

At that instant the lights on the tower flashed on again. The uniformed, helmeted figure in the distant tower waved a reassuring hand at him and said, "All clear!"

He thought the voice sounded funny, but he

didn't have much time to think about it, for suddenly the lights on his own tower began to flicker. Then they went out.

"They must be switching generators up at the power plant!" he yelled. "Now mine are on the fritz!"

"They'll come on again," the man in the other tower told him.

The German frowned. That voice! The strange accent! It came to him with a shock. The man in the other tower was not his friend Erich! He reached once again for the telephone to alert headquarters. But it was too late.

Craig Garrison came over the side of the box like a panther, 180 pounds of muscle and fury. The German chopped at Garrison's throat with the side of his hand. Garrison blocked the blow with an elbow and sliced the German across the bridge of his nose with a deadly karate blow. The battle was over.

Garrison vaulted over the side of the box and

166

landed lightly on the soft earth below. Goniff was already at work on the heavy lock that barred them from the dam and reservoir. He picked it in three minutes flat and flung open the gate. Garrison walked to the rim of the reservoir and took the bottle from his pocket. He unscrewed the cap and let the thick, milky liquid trickle into the water.

At the laboratory, General Schwartz, Colonel Dorne, and a squad of Gestapo men were questioning Casey and Kati. They still had no idea that she was really Emily Kropotkin.

"Where is your twin sister?" growled Werner, the blond Gestapo guard who had been tied up in the closet.

"She has no sister, you fool!" Casey laughed. "Can't you get it through your thick skull that it was *me* impersonating Kati? She had nothing to do with it at all." He pointed to the woman's clothing and the blond lady's wig that still lay in a corner of the room where he had discarded them. "There's your proof."

"He's telling the truth, I think," said the lieutenant who had been officer of the guard that night. "Kati is only a feebleminded peasant girl. She has been doing our laundry and sewing for the past year. She is too simple to be a part of this scheme. The American spies have used her as a dupe."

"Maybe so." General Schwartz turned away from the girl and glowered at Casey, who was bound to a chair with heavy rope.

"Where are your friends?" he demanded.

"I have no friends," Casey lied. "I was a bomber pilot. My plane was shot down and I've been trying to work my way back to England." He grinned. "Only my compass was broke and I went the wrong way and ended up in Prague. Bad mistake!"

"Swine!" the general roared. He slapped Casey viciously.

"We know who you are," Colonel Dorne said. "You and your friends have the whole countryside in an uproar. You have caused more trouble than an entire American division could have done."

"Garrison's Gorillas!" exclaimed a Gestapo officer.

"Who else?" General Schwartz sighed and mopped his face with a handkerchief. When the *Führer* found out all that had happened this terrible night, he would fly into one of his fits and foam at the mouth. He shook his fist in Casey's face.

"Before this night is over you will tell us where the rest of the Americans are hiding! You will tell us the names of the Czechs in the underground who helped you in this adventure. And you will most certainly tell us where they have taken Professor Kropotkin."

The Gestapo men took off their coats and rolled up their sleeves. They put on brass knuckles, and some of them armed themselves with short clubs.

Kati turned her eyes away and shut them very tightly. She had watched the Gestapo torture men before.

13.

DON'T DRINK ANYTHING!

ONE OF THE Gestapo men drew back his fist to strike Casey. He hesitated as he heard the sound of loud talking and footsteps in the hall outside the laboratory. The sergeant of the guard entered the room and saluted.

"Excuse the interruption, please, but we have another prisoner out here."

"Bring him in," the general said.

Two soldiers shoved Goniff through the doorway and stepped back.

172

"He came up to the gate with his hands in the air and said he wanted to surrender."

"What I said was that I wanted to make a deal," Goniff corrected him.

Both General Schwartz and Colonel Dorne spoke English. General Schwartz questioned Goniff.

"What kind of a deal?"

"I'm sick of this rotten job," Goniff told him. "The only reason I joined Garrison's suicide outfit was to get out of jail. I got to thinking that maybe the Germans could offer me a better deal— in exchange for certain information."

Casey struggled against the ropes that bound him. His face was white with anger. "You lousy rat!" he shouted at Goniff. "An old pro like you wouldn't turn stool pigeon!"

"Cool off, Casey." Goniff walked over to him and stood with his hands on his hips. "Get wise, fella. What do any of us owe to Garrison or the United States?"

173

"Goniff!" Casey roared. "So help me, I'll kill you if I ever get the chance."

The Germans were enjoying the argument between the two Americans. General Schwartz rubbed his plump hands together eagerly.

"Yes, yes, my dear fellow, I am sure we can offer you a much better deal than you have been getting. But first I would have to know what kind of information you can give us."

"Well, it's this way," Goniff said. "You guys are after some kind of formula, right?"

All of the Germans were gathering around him now. Schwartz asked, "You will take us to where this Garrison and his Gorillas are holding Professor Kropotkin?"

"Naw! I can't do that. The last I saw of them they were heading south in a stolen German command car."

The general swung around to Colonel Dorne. "Get that on the radio at once! Alert everyone to be on the lookout for them."

"You don't need to worry about them, General," Goniff said, grinning. "What do you need Jules Kropotkin for? You already know the part of the formula that he has. Right?"

"Yes, but—"

"No 'buts' about it. The person you want is the one that has the other part of the formula."

"Yes—his brother Emile," said the general. "You can take us to where Emile is hiding?"

Goniff began to laugh. "His brother Emile! Some joke!"

"What joke? What are you talking about?" the general demanded impatiently.

"Jules Kropotkin ain't got no brother!" Goniff announced. He turned and looked at Kati.

"What nonsense!" snapped Colonel Dorne. "This man doesn't know anything, General. He is just stalling for time. I say we shoot him and forget him."

"No, wait," General Schwartz said. "Why do you say that Jules Kropotkin has no brother?"

175

Goniff smiled. "There is no *Emile* Kropotkin. But there is an *Emily* Kropotkin. They were a brother and sister team, but they fooled you Germans real good—even switched birth certificates to throw you off the trail. All this time you been looking for a guy when you should have been looking for a girl."

"Ridiculous!" Colonel Dorne said.

"Maybe. Maybe not," said the general. "If what you say is true, where is this Emily Kropotkin?"

Goniff pointed to the laundry girl. "Right there. You know her as Kati. But her real name is Emily Kropotkin, and she has the other half of the formula you want."

If the Germans had any doubts about the truth of what Goniff had told them, they all disappeared when the girl turned pale, moaned, and toppled off her chair in a dead faint. The general ordered the soldiers to carry the unconscious woman into the little sewing room across from the laboratory.

"Put these two in there with her under heavy guard," he said, indicating Goniff and Casey.

"You ain't going to untie him, are you?" Goniff pointed to Casey. "He said he'd kill me. You heard him."

The general sneered. "Then it will save us the trouble. Get rid of them," he told the soldiers.

Emily Kropotkin, Goniff, and Casey were removed to the little room and two guards with submachine guns were stationed outside the door. As soon as they were alone Casey advanced on Goniff with blood in his eye, gingerly touching his wrists, which were rubbed raw from the ropes.

"You rotten traitor!" he said bitterly. "You stoolie! How could you do it, Goniff? I always thought you were a good Joe."

"It's okay, Casey," Goniff whispered to him. "It was a put-up job, me turning myself in. Garrison's orders."

Casey's jaw dropped. "Huh?"

"I had to get a message in to you and her." He

177

indicated the girl, who was starting to regain consciousness. "I had to warn you. *Don't drink anything!* Water, coffee, anything they serve you. Don't drink it. We put the Kropotkin formula, the Fear One-X, into their drinking water supply. How about that!"

"Good night!" Casey was jolted. "And her—was it on the level about her being Kropotkin's sister?"

"Sure it was. I had to tell them to buy time, or they would have tortured us—maybe even killed us. This way, the heat will be off us for a while—long enough, at least, for that serum to start taking effect. They have what they want. Or they think they do."

He bent over Emily Kropotkin and slapped her cheeks gently to bring her out of the daze. "Miss. Miss Kropotkin. Listen to me very carefully. If you do what we tell you, everything is going to be all right."

She sat up straight and shook her head. "I—I

178

don't understand, but I will try. What do you want me to do?"

A half hour later the three prisoners were escorted back into the laboratory. General Schwartz looked very pleased with himself. He clicked his heels and bowed to the girl.

"There is no use in pretending, Miss Kropotkin," he said. "We know who you are. Now you can save us all a lot of trouble if you cooperate with us. We want the other half of the formula you and your brother developed for the serum Fear One-X. You won't be sorry, I promise you, if you help us willingly. After Germany is victorious, all of us—yes, even Adolf Hitler himself—will be grateful to you. We will even forgive your brother for going off with the Americans."

Emily hung her head sorrowfully. "All right. What else can I do? You can have the formula. . . . It will take me several hours to put it all down on paper, you understand. And I will have to consult

Jules's notebooks to refresh my memory."

"Yes, of course." The general pointed to the shelves of books and notebooks above the desk where Jules Kropotkin had worked during his imprisonment. "Everything is there, Miss Kropotkin. You will get to work immediately."

He turned to Colonel Dorne. "This is going to be a long night," he said. "Have Bertha prepare coffee and sandwiches for us. Yes, and for the men on duty. Lots of good coffee."

Casey and Goniff exchanged a silent look of satisfaction. *Lots of coffee!* Coffee meant water. And water meant that the Fear 1-X would be working its way slowly and surely through the pipes from the reservoir.

"What about these two?" asked one of the Gestapo men, glaring at Casey and Goniff.

General Schwartz shrugged. "Put them under guard. Tomorrow we will have them shot as spies and saboteurs."

The clock on the wall read 1:35 A.M. Was there

enough time? Casey wondered.

As they left the room Goniff flashed a warning look at Emily. She understood what he meant.

Don't drink anything!

14.

AT BALZER'S
COTTAGE

Back at Balzer's hut, Craig Garrison and his men waited and watched the clock. Jules Kropotkin paced up and down nervously.

"It must work," he muttered. "It *has* to work!"

The Chief and Casino were playing poker in a corner of the underground communications room. "It kind of brings back memories, don't it?" Casino asked. "Like the night before you pulled off a big job. I never could sleep."

The Chief just grunted and fingered the leather

garrote fastened to his belt.

The Actor stretched. "Now, for my part, I always slept like a baby before a big caper."

Craig Garrison grinned and shook his head. They were some bunch, his Gorillas. He wondered what they would do when they went back to civilian life. *If* they went back! It was a big "if"! Tonight could be the end of everything for all of them.

The thought had no sooner formed in his mind than one of the lookouts stationed around the outside of Balzer's cottage came running down the ladder breathlessly.

"A German patrol! At least twenty men! They're coming this way!"

"Lights out and everybody quiet!" Balzer said. He and the lookout went up the ladder and closed the hidden door in the floor. They just had time to put the rug and table in place over it when there was a violent knocking on the door of the cottage.

"Out the back window!" Balzer hissed to the other man. Then he yelled out as the knocking was repeated, "Yes, yes! I'm coming!"

He walked to the door and opened it. A sergeant and two soldiers stood on the steps. Behind them were many more soldiers. The sergeant was a Nazi he recognized from the big army camp in the valley. In the winter Balzer supplied the barracks with firewood.

"Good evening, Balzer!" the German snapped. "You're up late, aren't you?" His suspicious eyes climbed up from Balzer's feet to his head. "And fully clothed, too," he added.

"I took some wood to the old woman up the road," he said. "She's sick. She says the Germans took the girl Kati away."

"That is none of your business," the sergeant snapped. He and the two privates on either side of him pushed Balzer aside and entered the cottage. The privates searched the small bedroom and pantry and in the cupboards.

Balzer laughed. "What are you looking for? Mice and cockroaches? You are welcome!"

The sergeant glared at him. "No jokes. Have you seen any strangers in the area this evening?"

"No. Why, is there some trouble?" Balzar said innocently.

The sergeant looked around the room thoughtfully. "There is always something happening in this sector. We think there is an unlawful radio transmitter around here as well."

Balzer shrugged and yawned. "I wouldn't know about such things. Now, *Herr* Sergeant, if you will be so kind—it is very late, and I am tired."

The sergeant nodded to his men and the three Germans moved toward the door. They were just about to leave when the door burst inward and three soldiers shoved a man in peasant dress into the room. It was Balzer's friend, the resistance fighter who had left through the rear window.

"We found this swine hiding in the backyard," one of the soldiers growled.

The sergeant glared at Balzer. "Do you know him?"

"Of course," Balzer said. "It is Anton. He is very shy."

"Oh, is he!" the sergeant roared. He hit Balzer across the mouth with the back of his hand, then snapped his fingers at the soldiers. "I don't trust these two. Something funny is going on. Tear this room apart!"

One of the Germans kicked over the table and another flung the rug to one side. They almost missed seeing the trapdoor, it was so skillfully camouflaged. It was the sergeant who got down on his knees and ran the tips of his fingers over the rough floorboards.

"Wait a minute," he said. "I think—yes, I know it is! A trapdoor! Kraus, your bayonet!"

He drove the tip of the bayonet under one corner of the door and lifted. All at once the door was flung open from below, slamming the sergeant in the face. The head and shoulders of the

Chief emerged, the long knife held between his teeth. He hurled himself at the closest soldier. The German screamed and tried to bring up his rifle, but the Indian's knife struck first.

The rest of Garrison's Gorillas came pouring out of the hole, their German carbines blazing. Balzer leaped to the door and slammed the thick steel bolt. Outside, the other soldiers, bewildered by the shooting, were pounding on the door and yelling, "Open up or we'll break it down!"

The reply from inside was a fusillade of bullets through the wood. The Germans scattered, and a corporal issued sharp orders.

"Surround the place. Don't expose yourself to their fire. We'll radio the camp for reinforcements. . . . Yes, and one tank."

Inside, Garrison and his band doused the lights and took up positions at the windows. The six Germans who had been inside the hut were all accounted for. Their bodies were lying in the room below, where Professor Kropotkin sat staring sadly at his clasped hands.

"It's no use," he said. "Something has gone wrong. The serum is not working."

"It's too early to tell, Professor," Garrison called down to him. "We won't know for certain until morning."

"That will be too late for us," Kropotkin said.

Garrison had no ready answer for that. The German bullets were flying over their heads as thick as bees.

At the German camp in the valley, the communications center was having a busy night.

"More reinforcements," a tired radio operator groaned. "If this keeps up, there won't be a man left in camp."

"What is it this time?" a lieutenant snapped.

"Balzer the woodcutter's cottage. Something is happening there. They want more men and a tank. It may be they have the American saboteurs trapped."

In the barracks lights flashed on and sleeping men were aroused out of bed. They staggered into the latrine to wash their sleepy eyes with cold water. Many of them took a cool drink as well.

The soldiers going on duty went to the mess hall, where the cooks were brewing fresh tea and coffee. Canteens were filled with fresh water. The detail moved out with a single tank leading the way.

Back at Balzer's cottage, Casino spotted the arrival of the reinforcements first. "They got a tank with them. I guess this is curtains for us."

Minutes later the siege began. The tank rumbled into Balzer's front yard, crushing the wood rail fence. Its heavy machine guns tore a gaping hole in the side of the hut. There was nothing the men inside could do against this steel monster. They flattened themselves on the floor and waited for death.

190

Then it happened!

Just as the tank seemed about to crash into the hut, it stopped short. Then the turret burst open and the tank's crew scrambled out and fled into the darkness, screaming in panic.

"What the devil!" Balzer said.

Garrison got up and rushed to a window. "The serum! The Fear One-X! It's working!" He pumped three shots at the fleeing Germans from the window.

One of them narrowly missed a German soldier crouching in the road. He stared in horror at the spot where the bullet had struck. He began to tremble and dropped his gun. A corporal ran up to him.

"Schultz, what is wrong with you? Pick up your rifle!"

The soldier shook his head and backed off, covering his face with his hands. "No! No! I'm getting out of here!" He screamed and ran.

The corporal rallied the other men. "Charge!"

he commanded and started running toward the house. Only a few soldiers followed him. Halfway across the yard gunfire erupted from the house. The corporal saw a man drop alongside him. Suddenly he was gripped by such intense fear that he thought he would faint. He had never experienced anything like it in his whole life. Turning around, he, too, fled in panic back into the woods.

The whole Nazi force was crumbling.

"Let's go!" Garrison led his men out of the house. "Into the tank!" Garrison, Casino, and the Actor climbed inside to operate it. The Chief and Balzer and his men rode on the outside like a bunch of cheering firemen on their way to put out a blaze.

Now the German tank turned its guns back on its owners. Only a few Nazi soldiers were still around to fight. A mere handful of them had not been dosed with the contaminated water from the reservoir. These few were quickly finished off or sent fleeing in full retreat.

The Gorillas and their underground allies stopped long enough to get Professor Kropotkin. Then Garrison gunned the tank along the dirt road that led to the chalet where Casey, Goniff, and Emily Kropotkin were imprisoned.

On the way they passed a roadblock. The German soldiers who manned it were all huddled in the road, weeping and shivering like frightened children. At the approach of the roaring tank carrying Garrison and his wild crew, they ran off into the woods.

A little farther on they came upon two armored cars abandoned in the middle of the road. A lone German soldier was crouched under the front seat of one of the cars.

Craig Garrison felt the hairs at the back of his neck tingling. He turned to the Actor in the seat beside him.

"Makes you think, doesn't it?"

The Actor arched his eyebrows. "Makes you

think about what, warden?"

Professor Kropotkin gave the answer for him. "Can you imagine what would have happened to the world if the Nazis had captured Emily and me together? They would have had the formula nineteen months ago. They would have enslaved the peoples of every continent and nation by now. Adolf Hitler would be king of the world."

"That's a frightening idea, all right," the Actor said.

"Don't go counting our chickens just yet," Casino reminded them. "We still ain't sure that those Jerries guarding the lab have been drugged up with Fear One-X."

"That is true," Kropotkin agreed. He looked very solemn. "Remember, too, they have Emily. The complete formula is in their hands now."

Garrison advanced the tank's throttle as high as it would go.

15.

THE MIGHTY MEN

CASEY AND GONIFF kept looking out of the window of the room where they were imprisoned. They had a good view of the double gates in front of the house. In the glare of the spotlights, it was as bright as day. Everything seemed perfectly normal. The gate guards paced back and forth. From time to time the sentries patrolling the perimeter of the fence strolled into view, their submachine guns slung over their shoulders.

The soldiers who were posted outside the door

of the room seemed normal, too.

"Maybe that stuff doesn't work," Casey whispered. "Maybe it's lost its strength."

Goniff shook his head. "I don't think these characters have had anything to drink."

He walked to the door and opened it. "Hey, you guys," he said. "Ain't it customary when somebody gets executed to give him anything he wants to eat and drink?"

One of the Germans spoke English. "What do you want?" he asked.

"Just some sandwiches and coffee."

The guard called the sergeant who was stationed at the foot of the stairs and repeated Goniff's request. The sergeant asked Colonel Dorne.

"Why not?" the colonel said. "I think I could use a sandwich myself."

A while later the guard returned with a tray of sandwiches and coffee. Goniff and Casey each took a sandwich and a cup of coffee.

"That's plenty for us," Goniff said. He gave

the rest of the sandwiches and coffee to the Germans. "You guys can have the rest."

The Nazis shrugged and dug into the food and drink with greedy hands. Casey winked at Goniff. They went back into the room and poured their coffee into a flowerpot standing on the windowsill.

Across the hall, Emily Kropotkin was having her own troubles. The coffee that had been served almost a half hour earlier sat untouched on the table. General Schwartz kept hovering over her shoulder as she put down the complicated equations on the notepaper in front of her.

"I'm so tired," she said finally, putting her head down in her hands.

"You must not fall asleep, Miss Kropotkin," the general said anxiously. He snapped an order at one of the three Gestapo men who were stationed in the lab. "Pour Miss Kropotkin a cup of coffee."

Emily lifted her head and smiled. "Will you

join me, General? I hate to drink alone."

He frowned. "I hate coffee. It keeps me awake. However, I will keep you company with a bottle of beer. Send down for some bottles of beer," he ordered.

Emily left her coffee cup untouched on the desk beside her.

A few minutes later the Gestapo man who had gone downstairs for the beer burst into the room excitedly.

"*Herr* General!" he said breathlessly. "Something strange is going on. The men downstairs—you will not believe this but they have put their weapons in a closet."

Schwartz's eyes bulged. "Put their weapons in a closet! What on earth for?"

The man gulped. "They say they are afraid of guns. A couple of them cried like children when I spoke to them too loudly."

General Schwartz looked around wildly. "Oh, no!" he gasped. "It can't be!" He rushed over to the desk and pulled Emily Kropotkin around roughly.

"Why aren't you drinking your coffee?" he demanded.

Her face was pale. "I—I have had some of it. It's cold. I don't like cold coffee."

He put his finger into the cup and pulled it out quickly. "You lie! The coffee is steaming!" He picked up the cup and held it out to her. "Drink it!" he ordered.

Emily shook her head.

"Why not?"

She said nothing.

The general's face grew beet red. "I'll tell you why you won't drink it!" he said. "It is contaminated, isn't it? Somehow the American dogs have found a way to put the fear serum into our water supply! Haven't they?"

She shook her head and cringed. "I don't know anything about it. How could it be possible? There is no serum as yet!"

"But there *is!*" the general raged. "Or there was! Your brother took the only supply of it away from this laboratory when he escaped!"

He slapped his head and groaned. "The reservoir! That must be it! Werner! Werbel!" he spoke to the Gestapo men. "Hurry! Warn everyone not to drink a drop of anything."

At that instant the door opened and Casey and Goniff leaped into the room. They were armed with the guards' submachine guns. Behind them in the hall General Schwartz saw the two German soldiers cringing back against the wall with their arms around each other. They were crying like babies.

The Gestapo men went for their pistols. Two shots splintered the doorjamb alongside Casey's head. He squeezed off a burst of machine-gun fire. Two of the Germans were slammed against the wall in back of them like rag dolls. The third raised his hands.

"I surrender!" he shouted.

"Well, I *don't!*" General Schwartz dragged the girl out of her chair and swung her in front of him as a shield. He drew his Luger.

"Put down those machine guns!" he ordered, "or I'll kill Miss Kropotkin!"

Casey looked helplessly at Goniff.

"We got no choice," Goniff said. He bent over to lay down his weapon.

Along the way to the chalet, Garrison's Gorillas picked up an assortment of resistance fighters. They leaped aboard the tank, and when there was no more room, they ran alongside.

"We have waited a long time for this day," Balzer said.

Garrison grinned. "It's not the end of the war, my friend."

"No, but it is the beginning of the end," the Czech underground leader said. "I feel it in my bones. The Nazi monster is beginning to fall apart. A little here. Tomorrow a little in France.

Then the Allied armies will storm ashore, and it will be over."

"I wish I had your confidence," Garrison said. "All right, here we go, men. Just around the bend!"

The men on the outside of the tank jumped off and deployed along the sides of the road.

The Fear 1-X serum was beginning to work on the German soldiers guarding the laboratory. Some of them were already reduced to shaking hulks of jelly. At the appearance of Garrison and his screaming band, they dropped their guns and ran. Others who had drunk the contaminated water or coffee at a later hour still were not feeling the full effect. They exchanged gunfire with the attackers briefly. A few fell. Then the terror gripped them, too, and they screamed for mercy. The battle was short.

Garrison drove the tank straight through the fence, leaving Balzer and his men to round up German prisoners. From around each side of

the house came a Nazi tank to intercept him. Their machine guns and cannons zeroed in on Garrison's tank. Slugs clanged off the steel plates. A shell took the top of the turret away.

"Wow!" Casino shouted above the racket. "That was too close for comfort!" He triggered off a shot from their cannon. It exploded on the front of the lead tank, just above the driver's observation port.

"Bull's-eye!" Garrison cried. "Good shooting, Casino!"

The German tank went out of control and zig-zagged around the yard, smoke and flames streaming from it.

That was too much for the crew of the other tank. The Fear 1-X reached a critical point in their bodies. They turned around and fled as fast as the tank would go. The last Garrison saw of them was as the tank crashed through the back fences and lost itself in the woods.

Garrison braked the tank at the front steps of

the house, and they all piled out. The front door stood wide open, and the guard was gone. Inside they came upon an eerie scene. German soldiers hid behind chairs and sofas, sniveling and shaking. There was no resistance whatsoever. Garrison, the Chief, the Actor, and Casino ran up the stairs and down the hall to the laboratory.

They skidded to an abrupt stop, almost tripping over each other. Casey and Goniff were standing at one side of the door inside the room with their hands raised. There were two dead Gestapo men against the far wall. A third Gestapo man was covering Casey and Goniff with a submachine gun. And behind the desk stood General Schwartz, with Emily Kropotkin in front of him. His Luger pistol was pressed against her side, under her heart.

"That's far enough!" Schwartz said sharply. "Drop your weapons, or the girl dies!" His finger tightened on the trigger.

Garrison nodded to his men. "Do as he says."

He sensed that the German general was serious and desperate.

Grumbling, they did as Schwartz ordered.

"Now, over there against the wall!" the general said. He edged toward the door, still holding the woman in front of him.

"You won't get far," Garrison warned him.

"We will see about that," Schwartz sneered. He backed slowly out the doorway, still covering Emily with the Luger. To the Gestapo man with the machine gun he said, "Now, Werner! Kill them all!"

The blond German brought up the muzzle of the submachine gun. Suddenly there was a loud outcry from General Schwartz. He pushed Emily away from him and fell forward on his face. A bayonet was embedded in his back.

And standing behind him in the hallway was Jules Kropotkin. His face was very white, but his voice was strong.

"Murderer!" He spat on the fallen general.

"I've wanted to do that for these nineteen long months."

The Gestapo man with the machine gun turned his head an instant to look at his general, and in that instant the Chief's right hand flashed through the air so fast that it was a blur. The long knife crossed the room like a streak of light. Werner screamed once and clutched at the deadly blade. Then his knees gave way and he collapsed.

Emily Kropotkin ran into her brother's arms.

"Jules!" she cried. "I never thought I'd see you again."

"It's all right, my dear." He patted her back. "Everything is all right now."

"Not quite," Garrison said grimly. "We have to get to the underground's airstrip now."

Balzer appeared. His face was smiling. "You will have a military escort to see that you get there safely." He stepped aside, and into the room paraded a troop of Czech underground fighters all dressed in captured Nazi uniforms.

Ten minutes later they were on their way. Garrison's Gorillas and the professor and his sister rode inside the car. The disguised resistance fighters led the way on German motorcycles with sirens screaming.

Several times on the way the procession forced other vehicles off the road. There were dozens of abandoned cars and other military equipment. Bands of terrified German soldiers were wandering around aimlessly under the effects of Fear 1-X.

"The entire German Army in this sector is helpless," Jules Kropotkin said. He patted his sister's arm. "Well, the Nazis wanted a big test of the formula. Hitler wanted it. Now they have their wish."

Garrison laughed. "Only we turned the tables on them. Instead of Americans, Englishmen, and Frenchmen whimpering on their knees and asking for mercy, it's German soldiers."

"Nazi supermen!" Casino whooped. He popped his head out of the car and stared at a

miserable-looking German soldier who was cling-
ing to a tree.

At the underground's secret airstrip a twin-
engine transport was waiting for them, its engines
idling. Garrison was the last one to board the
plane.

He turned and shook hands warmly with
Balzer. "Thank you, my friend. We could not
have done it without you and your men."

The Czech laughed and tugged at his beard.
"After the war, in years to come, when we are old
and gray, we will sit around the fire at night and
tell our grandchildren about the deeds done by
you and your mighty men. It will live forever in
our hearts, the legend of Garrison's Gorillas."

When the plane was airborne, Craig Garrison
spoke to his men. "You heard what Balzer said.
We may end up as Czech national heroes. Don't
you ever forget it. A hero has something to
measure up to—a responsibility to his fellowman.

If we ever get out of this war alive, and I ever read about any one of you jokers getting in trouble with the law again, I'll come and personally wring his no-good neck. Understand?"

The Chief, the Actor, Casino, Casey, and Goniff looked at each other with sheepish grins. They mumbled their replies.

"Yes, sir."

"Sure, Lieutenant."

"We read you."

Garrison was happy. Not one of them had called him "the warden."

Whitman
CLASSICS

Pinocchio

Stand By for Adventure

Alice in Wonderland

Black Beauty

Tales to Tremble By

Heidi

Little Women

Tales From Arabian Nights

Huckleberry Finn

The Call of the Wild

Tom Sawyer

Robin Hood

The Wonderful Wizard of Oz

Robinson Crusoe

Wild Animals I Have Known

The War of the Worlds

Here are some of the best-loved stories of all time. Delightful ... intriguing ... never-to-be-forgotten tales that you will read again and again. Start your own home library of WHITMAN CLASSICS so that you'll always have exciting books at your fingertips.

Whitman

REG. U.S. PAT. OFF.

Whitman ADVENTURE and MYSTERY Books

Adventure Stories for GIRLS and BOYS...

BRAINS BENTON SERIES
The Missing Message
The Counterfeit Coin
The Stolen Dummy

DONNA PARKER
In Hollywood
Special Agent
On Her Own
A Spring to Remember
Takes a Giant Step

POWER BOYS SERIES
The Haunted Skyscraper
The Flying Skeleton
The Burning Ocean
The Million-Dollar Penny
The Double Kidnapping
The Vanishing Lady

REAL LIFE STORIES
To Dance, To Dream
Heroes in Blue and Gray

New Stories About Your Television Favorites...

Bonanza

The Man From U.N.C.L.E.
The Gentle Saboteur
The Gunrunners' Gold

F Troop

The Gnome-Mobile

Lassie
Secret of the Summer
Blackberry Bog
Bristlecone Pine

I Spy

The Munsters
The Last Resort

Gilligan's Island

The Big Valley

The Green Hornet

Tarzan

Walt Disney's Annette